T0007319

For the Love of Rachel

Sally Campbell Repass

authorHOUSE®

AuthorHouse™
1663 Liberty Drive
Bloomington, IN 47403
www.authorhouse.com
Phone: 1-800-839-8640

First published by AuthorHouse 7/9/2010

ISBN: 978-1-4520-4177-3 (e)
ISBN: 978-1-4520-4176-6 (sc)

Printed in the United States of America
Bloomington, Indiana

This book is printed on acid-free paper.

THIS BOOK IS DEDICATED TO...

Paul, my Wonderful Husband of 8 years, who has stood by me through all the phases of this book. He has been my inspiration.

To my Wonderful Children... Tony, Tammy, Travis, Tracy, Trent & Bob
To their Spouses... Kari, Jennifer & Lori

To my Special Grandchildren... Jessica, Katie, Campbell, Robert, Justin, Nick & Matthew

In Loving Memory of my Wonderful Parents...
Warren & Ethel Aker Campbell...
GONE BUT NOT FORGOTTEN

Chapter 1

She sat staring out the window. Rachel Hargrove Parker knew something was wrong. She felt it in the pit of her stomach. Her husband Mitch, was two hours late. He was never this late... Something had happened to him... she just knew. "Dear God... Please let him be alright," she prayed.

The rain beat gently upon the window pane and glistened from the outside light. She always turned the light on for him each evening. This was to let him know she welcomed him home. She had done this since the beginning of their marriage five years ago. She wanted him to know how much she loved him and that she was waiting with open arms.

But tonight, somehow seemed different. She was so anxious to see him, but had a bad feeling... This was a feeling unlike any she had ever had before. She looked at the clock. The minutes were ticking by so slowly. She kept watching for his headlights to come up the driveway. Suddenly, she saw car lights and a surge of relief flooded her body.

The car came closer... she could see a light on the top. It was not Mitch, but a police car instead. She felt her heart drop! Panic set in... Two policemen got out of the car and started toward the house. This could only mean one thing. It brought back memories to her of when she was ten years old. That time, they brought news that her parents had been killed in a car wreck. How could she go through this again? She couldn't stand it any longer, and ran out the door into the rainy damp night. The rain was hitting her in the face, but she felt nothing. She was too numb with fear. This was a living nightmare! It couldn't be happening to her again. She couldn't lose the love of her life.

They had only been married five years, and that was such a short time. Those had been the most wonderful years of her life. How could she face life without him? How could "they" face life without him? Yes, she had planned to tell him tonight. She had gone to the doctor today, and he had confirmed her pregnancy. She was so happy it had finally happened. They had been trying to have a baby from the beginning of their marriage. She was very excited and knew Mitch would be, too. She had planned a special dinner for him, with candlelight and roses.

Reality set in... the policemen were getting closer. "Hello Rachel," said the short stocky one, named Dan. "May we go inside and talk?" Tears welled up in her eyes, as she turned and headed for the door. He didn't have to tell her... she already knew what he was going to say. Without saying a word, she opened the door, and took a step inside the beautiful home she shared with her loving husband, Mitch. The policemen followed her in. "Please Dear God," she was praying, "don't take my loving husband from me. It took us so long to find each other again. I need him so much!"

"Rachel," said the policeman, breaking her chain of thoughts. "There's been an accident." Rachel stared at him, as if he wasn't even there. Shock had set in, and he hadn't even told her yet. Rachel was a smart girl, and figured it out without him saying a one word. Finally her gaze caught his and their eyes locked.

"I'm so sorry to have to tell you Rachel, but Mitch was in a terrible car accident on his way home. With the rain and slick roads, he was forced off the highway and down an embankment, by a big truck. He never survived the crash. He never felt any pain, as he died instantly," said policeman, Dan.

Rachel stared at him and anger filled her face. "Do you think that makes it any easier for me?" she asked angrily.

"I am so sorry," said the policeman. "There is no easy way to tell you. It is a tragic thing for sure."

"What can we do for you, Rachel?" asked Joe, the tall, slim policeman. "Can we take you to the hospital morgue? You will have to identify his body."

"No, thank you. I will drive myself," she said.

"Are you sure you are able to drive alone?" asked Dan.

"Yes, I will be okay," she stated.

"If there is anything we can do for you, don't hesitate to call," said Dan. The two men got up and let themselves out the door.

Rachel sat on the couch. She never bothered to get up and lock the door. What was she going to do? Not only was she alone now, but in seven months she would be a single mother. She was so sorry that Mitch never knew he was going to be a daddy. She was so excited about the baby, and couldn't wait for him to get home that night, so she could tell him the good news. But... he never came home!

She got up off the couch and went upstairs to freshen up. She came back down, picked up her umbrella, and walked out the door into the night. It was still raining and was quite foggy. She dreaded the drive... but even more what she was facing. She knew it had to be done... She arrived at the hospital about thirty minutes later. The rain had about stopped so she got out of her car, leaving her umbrella behind. She headed to the entrance, her body feeling numb all over. Her legs were barely holding her up. She kept telling herself, I have to be strong... I have to do this. Somehow she made it in the front door, as her head began to spin. A nearby nurse noticed her, and came over. "Lady, are you okay?' asked the nurse.

"No," whispered Rachel.

"How may I help you?" asked the nurse.

"I'm here to identify my husband. He was just killed," said Rachel, with her eyes full of tears. She couldn't hold them back.

"I am so sorry! What is your name?" asked the nurse.

"Rachel Parker," she replied.

"Was your husband Dr. Mitch Parker?" asked the nurse.

"Yes," she said in a whisper. "I can't believe this has happened."

"I'm sure you are still in shock. Did you drive yourself here?" asked the nurse.

"Yes," she whispered softly.

"You shouldn't have come alone," said the nurse.

"The policemen offered to drive me, but I wanted to come alone."

"Come on honey, I will take you downstairs."

Rachel followed her to the elevator. The door opened and they walked in. The nurse pushed the button for the basement, and down they went. The door opened and they walked out into a large room filled with gurneys. It was such a gruesome place. It had a strong smell of death. For a moment she thought she was going to be sick. Her head was spinning and she took hold of the nurse's arm. She wanted to turn and run... She wanted to get on the elevator, go back upstairs and run out into the night.

The coroner came over to meet them. "May I help you?" he asked.

Rachel just stood there with a lost look on her face, and never said a word. Seeing her state of mind, the nurse spoke up. "Mrs. Parker is here to identify the body of her husband, Dr. Mitch Parker, who was killed in a car accident a couple hours ago."

The nurse left them together and went back to her work upstairs.

"Yes, we do have him here," said the coroner. "I am so sorry for your loss, Mrs. Parker. Please follow me."

"Thank you," said Rachel in a faint voice.

The coroner stopped at the second table in the first row. He uncovered the body and Rachel gasped. The tears began to run down her cheeks. She leaned over and kissed him on the forehead. "Oh, Mitch," she cried." I can't give you up. I can't go on without you. You're too young to die. I am going to have your baby. I was going to tell you tonight. You can't leave us!!!" she sobbed and sobbed.

The coroner took her by the arm and pulled her away. She fell against him and cried until she had no tears left. He held and comforted her. Finally she pulled herself away, and apologized to him. "I'm sorry... I didn't mean to lose it like that, but this is the hardest thing I have ever had to face."

"You don't have to apologize, Mrs. Parker. I can understand what you are going through. I lost my wife several years ago. That was the most difficult thing I have ever been through. Believe me, I am truly sorry for your loss."

"Thank you for being so kind. I have to go now."

"Thank you for coming in so promptly," said the coroner. "May God Bless You!"

Rachel was crying so hard she couldn't even answer him. She found her way upstairs, and ran to the exit. She had to get out of there... She could hardly get her breath. Her heart was pounding wildly. It was raining again...She ran to her car, gasping for breath, as the rain pounded upon her head. She was too numb to feel anything. Her clothes were drenched and her sandals were soaked.

She unlocked her car and got in. She leaned over the steering wheel and let the tears flow. This was the worst night of her life. It felt like a nightmare. She kept hoping she would wake up and find it was not true. But she wasn't asleep and it was true. After several minutes, she regained her composure enough, to start her car and head for home.

The rain had slacked down by the time she reached home. She needed to talk to her foreman, Rex, but it would have to wait until morning. She was exhausted!

She walked in her house and locked the door behind her. The house was so quiet. It was too quiet! She walked over and turned on the TV. Anything to avoid the stillness of the night. She knew she needed to call Aunt Pat, but she dreaded so much to do that. She should have called her after the policemen left, but she just couldn't. She picked up the phone and dialed the number.

"Hello," said Aunt Pat.

"Aunt Pat," Rachel said in a trembling voice.

"What on earth is wrong?" asked her aunt. "Has something happened?"

"Yes," she answered so softly that her aunt could barely hear her.

"What has happened?" asked her aunt.

"It's Mitch," she said.

"Has something happened to Mitch?" asked Aunt Pat.

"Yes, he's dead."

"What??? What happened?" asked her aunt.

"He was killed in a car accident," she sobbed.

"Oh no...., I am so sorry, Rachel!" exclaimed her aunt. "I am coming over."

"Please wait until in the morning. I don't want you to drive on this rainy, dark night."

"Are you going to be okay by yourself?" she asked.

"I am okay. I have already been to the hospital morgue to identify his body. That was the hardest thing I have ever done in my life," she said in a faint voice.

"You should have called me. I would have gone with you," said Aunt Pat.

"If the weather hadn't been so bad, I would have called

you. That is why I waited until I got back to call you. I know how you are!"

"Well, I will be over in the morning for sure."

"I'll be looking for you. Thanks, Aunt Pat, and I love you!"

"You're so welcome. You know I will always be here for you. I love you, too, Rachel!" she exclaimed. "Try to get some sleep tonight."

"Good night, Aunt Pat. See you in the morning."

"Good night, dear Rachel." They both hung up their phones.

Aunt Pat was over early the next morning. Rachel was in the kitchen when she arrived. They had a cup of coffee together, but Rachel couldn't eat anything. She knew she needed to eat for the baby, but she couldn't stand the thought of food today.

"Aunt Pat, I have something exciting to tell you. Through all this grief, there is one bright spot. I am going to have a baby... Mitch's baby."

"Oh my goodness!" exclaimed Aunt Pat with joy.

"When did you find out?" she asked.

"Only yesterday, and I was going to tell Mitch last night. I fixed a special dinner for him, with candlelight and roses. It was supposed to be a joyous night for us, instead it turned into a tragedy. Oh, Aunt Pat... what am I going to do?"

"First of all, you are going to take care of yourself and the baby. I am going to stay with you for a couple weeks, and let you rest."

"You don't have to do that. I really appreciate all you

have done for me all these years, but I can't impose on you forever."

"I don't want to hear that. What I do for you is willingly and out of love for you. Don't ever think you are a burden," said Aunt Pat, with a heart full of love.

The next few days were a blur. Somehow she got through the funeral, but she felt like a zombie. Thank God for her church friends, and especially Aunt Pat. She could never have made it without her. But now she needed time alone, to grieve. She wanted to talk to no one. Friends kept coming by the house... she wished they would all go away, and leave her alone. She knew they meant well, but unless they had experienced a tragedy like this, they couldn't begin to understand. They kept telling her it would be okay, and she resented hearing that. Things would never be okay again. She hated them watching her and feeling sorry for her. She had to deal with this alone and in her own time.

Before Mitch died, they had discussed picking out a spot of land on the ranch for a family cemetery. They followed through with this idea, and did all the necessary paperwork, in order to make it the Parker Family Cemetery. She never dreamed they would be using it this soon. Mitch was buried there, and she would be buried next to him someday.

She had not worked since she and Mitch got married. He wanted her to stay home and start a family. Mitch was a doctor, and made a good living, so they could afford for her to stay home. She missed her co-workers at the medical clinic, but she had Mitch, so what more did she need, except to have his baby as soon as possible. But that never happened...until now, and he would never know. He was taken at such a young age, just thirty two. He was too young to die. They had too many plans that were left unfulfilled.

Rachel was a beautiful thirty two year old girl. She still considered herself a girl, even though she was no longer a teenager, or even in her twenties. She still had her long blonde hair, that was as soft as silk and looked like spun gold. She was tall, and slim, with the look of a model. Her face was as smooth as porcelain and her hazel eyes were the most beautiful eyes ever. She had great beauty inside and out. That's what attracted Mitch to her when they were in high school. He loved the beauty he saw within her, as well as her stunning looks.

Now he was gone, and she had to face life alone, without him. Five short, blissful years together, and it was over. That was much too soon! They had planned to grow old together. How would she keep up the big beautiful 2 story log home they had built together, in beautiful Laurel, Montana?

Chapter 2

She let her mind wander back to the time she was ten years old...

Aunt Pat had never married. She was engaged once to Roman Hunter, but he left her standing at the altar. He broke her heart so badly, that she vowed never to fall in love again, and she didn't. That was over thirty five years ago.

When Pat's older brother Tim, and his wife Sandy, had that horrible car accident that claimed their lives, she thought she would die, too! Tim was her only brother and all the family she had left. Their parents had died a few years earlier. Tim had always looked out for her, and now he was gone. She had loved him so much! Sandy was like a sister to her, also. She was going to be lost without them. So taking in their ten year old daughter Rachel, was not even questionable. Her home and her heart would always be home to Rachel. She was such a beautiful little girl and was not a spoiled brat like most young children her age.

Somehow, they made it through the funeral. Aunt Pat took Rachel home with her. They would grieve together, and try to move on. After all, life does go on. She had found that out, after Roman left her standing at the altar, all those many years ago. She grieved many years for him, and in time, the pain lessened. She still thought of him often, and probably always would. She knew she would never love anyone else. He had taken her heart when he left her.

Aunt Pat told Rachel they would redecorate her room. She could have it any way she wanted. That made Rachel happy. It brought a smile to her beautiful, yet sad, little face. So they were busy the next few weeks, choosing paint, wallpaper, curtains and a new bedspread. Aunt Pat could see the happiness in Rachel's eyes, and that was worth every penny she was spending.

Finally the room was finished and it was breathtakingly beautiful. Everything was done in pink. A beautiful room for a beautiful little girl. That seemed to be fitting. It made Aunt Pat happy to see how thrilled little Rachel was.

Summer was over and it was time for school. At least Rachel could start the first day of school, instead of the middle of the year The first few days were hard, but she adjusted well and soon made some new friends. It was always hard starting in a new school. Aunt Pat wished Rachel could have continued in the same school, but that was not possible, since they lived in the small town of Columbus, Montana... population 1, 748. Children adjust quickly and she felt sure Rachel would be alright. It would just take some time.

The years passed quickly. Rachel was very involved in school. She was a cheerleader in Middle School and High School. She participated in many different social activities, in and out of school. She was very popular, both with girls and boys. She was beautiful, but she never let it go to her head. She was friendly with everyone. She wasn't in a clique. She was always the same, no matter where she was at. Everyone loved her! That was probably one of the reasons she was voted Homecoming Queen in her Senior year. Voted King that year, was Mitch Parker, whom she started dating in her Junior year. Mitch had fallen in love with her at first sight. He thought she was the sweetest, most beautiful girl he had ever met.

Everyone knew Mitch planned to become a doctor. They knew he would be going off to college, somewhere far away. His dad had been a doctor also, and had left money to fund Mitch's education at Harvard in Boston. That was a world away from Montana. Would this be the end of Mitch and Rachel's romance? Only time would tell...

It was a sad day when Mitch went off to Harvard. Rachel couldn't hold back the tears, as he kissed her goodbye and boarded the plane for Boston. She felt so alone! She and Mitch had been inseparable since 11th grade. Now he was gone... He promised to write and call when he could. He would have a very heavy work load, so there wouldn't be much free time. He knew he would have to study hard, if he wanted to become a doctor and he was willing to make any sacrifice that he had to. Being a doctor had always been a dream of his. He wanted to follow in his father's footsteps.

The first month, Mitch wrote to her every week. She was always so excited, and would take his letter to her room and lay on the bed and read it. The second month the letters came a little less often. He did call her now and then, which really brightened her day. He could never talk very long, because he had so much to do. The conversations always seemed to be cut short. There was so much she wanted to tell him, but never had the time. By the end of the third month, the letters and phone calls ceased. Had she done something to make him mad? She couldn't think of anything. It all seemed to be over, and she was heartbroken! She moped around and finally Aunt Pat had a talk with her. She tried to explain that Mitch was busy with his studies, and probably didn't have time to write. But Rachel had known from his letters that things were not the same. At first he had told her how much he loved and missed her. Then later he talked about his work, and how he had no free time. She could feel him slipping away. But there was nothing she could do...

Aunt Pat told her not to worry. If they were meant to be together, God would work it all out. In her heart, she knew this was true, but it didn't make any sense to her now. Aunt Pat told her she needed to start dating and move on.

Chapter 3

Rachel had decided not to go to college. There was nothing left for college when her parents got killed. After the bills were paid, the money was gone. Anyway, she felt like she needed to get a job and help Aunt Pat with the expenses. Her aunt had been so good to her for the past eight years, since her parents died and this was the least she could do to help out.

She went for several interviews, before she landed a job in the local Medical Clinic as receptionist. She thought if she worked in the medical field, she would somehow feel closer to Mitch. So she was very happy when Columbus Medical Clinic hired her. She had gone for her interview on Thursday and would be going to work the following Monday. The clinic had three doctors... Dr. Moore, Dr. Lynch, and Dr. Jones, who would be retiring soon. A new doctor would replace him. The clinic was only five miles from where she lived with Aunt Pat.

Monday morning finally arrived, and off to work she went. Before leaving the house, she changed outfits three times. She wanted to make sure she looked professional, but not like a prude. She was introduced to the staff of nurses, as well as the doctors. Everyone seemed really nice and friendly. She was going to like it here. This would be good for her. She needed something to occupy her mind, other than thinking of Mitch all the time. It had been 8 years, and she was sure he had graduated by now. But she never heard from him, or anything about him. When he left Columbus, all memories of him left too, except for the ones Rachel had.

She had dated some during those eight years. She never fell in love with anyone. They all fell in love with her, but she couldn't make love happen for herself. It was either there, or it wasn't, and it never was for her.

She loved her new job! She made friends quickly. Her days were mostly spent answering the phone and making appointments. She was always very polite with the patients, whether it be on the phone or in person. She always had her winning smile for them as they approached her desk. She really loved the elderly people. They were very special to her. The patients learned to love her very quickly. They always looked forward to seeing her smiling face.

The girls in the office would set her up on a blind date, from time to time. She would rather they didn't, but never had the heart to tell them. Each time they would say, this may be the "one." But it never was. There would never be anyone for her, but Mitch and she had lost him years ago. It seemed life dealt her a cruel blow... she lost the ones she loved.

The girls really liked her and kept hoping they could find someone she would fall in love with. That never happened. There was always something missing and she could not

commit, unless things were exactly right. She would know...
She never went out with any of the guys more than twice.
She felt nothing except friendship for them, so she didn't
want to waste their time. None of them could compare to
Mitch. She knew she had to forget him, but that was easier
said than done.

One month later, Dr. Jones would be retiring. The office
girls were giving him a retirement dinner at the Columbus
Country Club on Saturday night. Rumor was that Dr. Jones'
replacement would be attending the dinner. All the girls,
except Rachel, were very excited. That was the talk around
the office. They wondered if he would be single, and would he
be good looking. The new doctor was the office buzz for a few
days. They had no idea how old he would be. Rachel thought
to herself... he might be old enough to be their father, too.
Then the joke would be on them. She never joined in on this
conversation. She would wait and see for herself.

The girls were all single, and decided they had to buy a
new dress for the dinner. Rachel didn't have the desire to go
shop for a new dress. She had plenty of pretty dresses in her
closet, and she would choose one of them. She would probably
wear the emerald green dress, that she had purchased a
couple years ago, for a church function. It brought out the
green in her eyes, and complimented her in every way. It was
a satin sheath, with an emerald pin on the large v-neck collar.
It looked very elegant. Every time she wore it, she always got
compliments.

Each of the girls bought a new dress, and this was
the topic of conversation in the office for the next week. It
seemed each one was trying to outdo the other. They asked

Rachel if she bought a new dress, and when she told them, no, they couldn't believe it. They wanted to know what she was wearing. When she told them ... just a dress she bought a couple years ago, the look on their faces, told exactly how they felt about that. Rachel had to smile to herself, when she thought of the gorgeous emerald green dress she would be wearing.

Chapter 4

Tonight was the dinner...She got off work at 5:00 o'clock and hurried home. She had two hours to get ready and get back to the Club.

Aunt Pat was in the kitchen preparing a salad when Rachel arrived home. "Would you like a salad?" she asked.

"Oh no, thank you. Did you forget I'm eating at the Country Club tonight?" asked Rachel.

Aunt Pat smiled and told her to have a good time. She said she wanted to hear all about it when she got home later that night.

Rachel was actually looking forward to tonight. It would be nice to get dressed up and have dinner at the Country Club with her co-workers. She was sorry to see Dr. Jones go, but she would soon get used to his replacement. As she had learned years ago, nothing lasts forever.

She slipped into the long emerald dress and matching shoes. Her makeup was immaculate, and her golden tresses were as smooth as silk. She said goodbye to Aunt Pat, but not before the click of the camera. She walked out the door and down the walk to where she had parked her red Mustang. It started right up and she was on her way.

It was a beautiful warm summer night. The sky was full of stars and a bright moon was shining. Rachel was feeling good. She drove the short distance to the Country Club, parked her car and got out. She walked up the front steps, and over to the door. As she entered, she saw her friends were already there. She stopped for a minute to observe them. Wow! They all looked beautiful! Molly was wearing a bright red dress. It was perfect with her long, straight, dark hair. Susan was wearing a royal blue dress, which matched her dark blue eyes, and looked stunning with her auburn curly hair. Lacy was wearing a pale pink dress, which was perfect with her blue eyes and short blonde hair. Jessica was wearing a sky blue dress, which made her eyes look even more blue. She looked absolutely gorgeous. Her dark blonde hair was in curls, and looked so perfect. Last of all, was Brooke... who was wearing a long black dress and looked very stunning. Her silver jewelry accented the black dress and made the look complete. Her blonde natural curly hair, was hanging in ringlets. All of them looked like models. Tonight, they looked so different from their every day "office look."

As she made her way farther into the room, everyone suddenly became quiet. All heads turned and all eyes were upon the beautiful Rachel. Time stood still... They had never seen anyone look so perfect... so much like a Goddess. Yet she had that innocent look about her, too. She smiled and said hello to everyone and joined the other girls.

A few minutes later, they went into the dining room and were seated. Dinner was about to be served... When suddenly, the front door opened and in walked the most handsome dark haired stranger. The girls all let out a "gasp." Rachel looked up, and thought her heart was going to stop beating. It couldn't be... but it was... Dr. Mitch Parker.

Dr. Moore and Dr. Lynch invited him to sit at the table with them, their spouses, and the "guest of honor." Where else would he sit? From time to time, Rachel would glance at him, but she made sure he never saw her looking. He seemed to be having a good time talking to the other doctors. One would never know that the two of them knew each other.

It was a wonderful meal, but her appetite was gone. Rachel kept thinking about Mitch. He had no woman with him, so that probably meant he wasn't married. She was surprised, and was sure it was his decision to stay single. She knew how women were. All of them would like to get their "claws" into this good looking doctor. She was sure of that. Mitch hadn't seen her yet, and she would like to keep it that way. She wished she could get out without being noticed, but she knew that wasn't possible. Even if it had been, she would be seeing him at work soon.

Suddenly he stood up, along with the other doctors. They were heading to her table. She could now see that he was not wearing a wedding band.

"Dr. Parker, I'd like for you to meet our office nurses." One by one, he introduced them to Dr. Parker. Each one gave him a polite hello and nice to meet you, while staring at this handsome hunk and thinking how lucky we are that he is coming to work at our office.

Last of all, he said, " This is our receptionist, Rachel Hargrove."

"Nice to meet you, Miss Hargrove." said Dr. Parker. His eyes locked with hers, and this made her very nervous. She was hoping that no one saw the look that passed between them. Would he mention that they already knew each other? She hoped not... She just wanted this to be over.

He soon turned away from their table and started talking to the other doctors, as if she were a stranger. Rachel felt a sigh of relief. It was better this way. She just wanted the night to be over.

Chapter 5

She dismissed herself early and left. What was supposed to have been a fun night, had turned to gloom, the minute he walked through that door. On the short drive home, he was all she thought about. How could he be over her so completely, and show no emotion, while she was dying inside? This was beyond her comprehension. Lord knows, she had tried to forget him. Even all those blind dates should have helped, but nothing worked. She found herself comparing him to each new guy that she met, and he always came out on top. None of them could ever measure up to Mitch. He had a terrible hold on her! She knew for certain, he was the Love of her Life... her Soul Mate. But she had lost him. Why did it have to hurt so badly? Now, here he was back, but something seemed different about him. He seemed tense, and not the same fun loving guy she had known in high school. I guess time changes us all, she thought.

She pulled into her driveway and got out of the car. Aunt Pat had left the porch light on for her. Brownie came bounding down the steps to meet her. She was so excited and wagging her tail. She was a spoiled little girl. Rachel had gotten her from the animal shelter about two years ago. Somehow Brownie knew she had been saved, and was forever loyal to her best friend. Rachel loved this little dog very much. Brownie was her friend, no matter what, and loved her unconditionally. That's how dogs are, she thought.

She walked up the front steps with Brownie at her heels. Once inside, Brownie headed for her bed. Aunt Pat was sitting on the sofa reading the paper. She was dying to hear about tonight, and the new doctor, but thought she would wait and let Rachel tell her.

"The new doctor is Mitch!" Rachel blurted out.

"You're kidding!" replied Aunt Pat in a surprised voice.

"I wish I was, but I'm not. It was so weird to see him again, after eight years. He has changed, Aunt Pat. He's not the same Mitch that I knew and loved. He seems to have hardened."

"He's a doctor now... maybe he's let that go to his head," said Aunt Pat.

"Maybe so," replied Rachel. "But I think he is still single."

"Really? I guess I am surprised about that. Well...only time will tell. If you two are meant to be together, God will work it all out... in His time, not yours," said Aunt Pat.

"I guess," said Rachel, not sounding too convincing. "I think I'll turn in. It's been a long stressful day. I need to get some extra rest, so I can get up and go to church in the morning. You do remember that I am doing the special?"

" I remember." said Aunt Pat.

They had been members of the Rose Baptist Church in

Columbus for many years. Rachel sings in the choir, and does specials when asked. She has always loved to sing. In fact, she started singing as a child.

Tomorrow is Easter Sunday, and Rachel planned to sing, 'Calvary', which is very fitting for this time of year. The church was always full on Easter Sunday. That was the only time some people ever came to church. It seemed so vain to only come then, just to show off your new Easter 'frock'. She often wondered how God felt about that.

After tossing and turning for an hour, Rachel finally went to sleep. She woke up several times during the night, and Mitch was always on her mind. The events of the night before, kept turning over and over in her mind. Finally the alarm on her clock buzzed at 7:00 a.m., and she jumped out of bed. What a long night it had been!

She went to the kitchen for a cup of coffee and a piece of toast. Aunt Pat was already up having her coffee, and reading the Sunday paper. They talked small talk as they sipped their coffee. After she finished her coffee and toast, she went to take a shower, and get ready for church.

She chose a pale pink dress, which looked great with her long blonde hair. Finally, she was ready to go, and looked rather stunning. She honestly didn't realize how beautiful she was, and that was a good thing. Usually women like that, let it go to their head... but not Rachel. Her Aunt Pat was always telling her how beautiful she was, but she knew the love her Aunt had for her, and guessed that was the reason. She loved her Aunt Pat so very much! She was the only family she had left.

The drive to the church was a lovely one. It was a warm

summer day, and the sun was shining brightly. The birds were singing, and butterflies were fluttering about. She felt so alive. After about ten minutes, they arrived at the church. The parking lot was almost full already. They found a space to park, even though they had to walk a fair distance. They got out of the car and headed toward the church. She had never seen so many fancy Easter frocks. Some women were wearing hats, and some weren't. She wasn't wearing one... In fact that was not her thing. Neither was Aunt Pat.

The organist was playing 'The Old Rugged Cross', as they walked in the front door. Such beautiful music to Rachel's ears! They found a seat about half way down the aisle on the right. People kept coming in. The church was indeed, going to be full this Easter Sunday morning.

Pastor Steve Weston had been at Rose Baptist Church for the past ten years. His congregation had grown to love him... and his wife, Kathy. She was a petite little woman, who always had a big smile and kind words for everyone. She was the perfect wife for a pastor. They were a perfect couple, and were always there if someone needed them.

Finally it was time for Rachel to sing the special. She left her seat in the choir, and went to the microphone. She spoke a few words, as she scanned the congregation from side to side. To her surprise, on the left, near the back, she saw Mitch. She felt panic about to set in, but she couldn't let him ruin her day. "Dear God," she prayed silently, "Give me the peace I need to sing this song of praise for you. In Jesus name I pray. Amen!" Suddenly she felt the hand of God touch her and the fear was gone. The music started and she sang like an angel. People were wiping their eyes and praising the Lord.

She glanced at Mitch, and saw he had a big smile on his face. She saw him wipe a tear from his eye.

When church was over, she found Mitch waiting for her outside. She could tell he was anxious. He was scanning the crowd, looking for her. At last he spotted her, and made his way over to where she was standing.

"Hi Rachel... it's good to see you again. You look breathtakingly beautiful and you have the voice of an angel. I didn't know you could sing so well," exclaimed Mitch.

"Thank you, Mitch. It's good to see you, too." I'm sure there's a lot about me that you don't know, she thought.

"I was so shocked to see you last night at the dinner, and I'm sorry if I acted like a jerk," he said. "You caught me off guard."

"It's okay. I was very surprised to see you, too! Looks like we will be seeing more of each other since we'll be working at the same clinic. I mean... professionally, that is. Well, I must run...and not keep Aunt Pat waiting."

"See you at work tomorrow," said Mitch.

"Sure," she answered.

She was very glad to get to the car. Her nerves were on edge. How dare he waltz in here, as if there had never been anything between them? Who does he think he is? Did he not know how much she had suffered because of him? He acted so innocent, and she would not give him the pleasure of knowing how he had hurt her. She was determined to keep that secret within her... and never let him know. Eight long years she had waited, without a word from him, after the first three months. There was no excuse for that kind of treatment. Maybe he never loved her as much as she loved him. That had to be the answer. Maybe now that she had seen him again, she could pick up the pieces and move on. Maybe this was the closure she needed. Time would tell...

Chapter 6

Monday morning came all too soon! Rachel never slept well last night. She dreaded going to work, for the first time since she went to work at the clinic. She waited until the last minute to leave the house. As she pulled into the parking lot, she saw a car she didn't recognize, It was a new white Infiniti convertible. Wow! It was a beautiful car. She knew that it had to belong to Mitch.

She walked into the office and took her seat behind the receptionist desk. She wondered how long it would be before she saw him. She didn't have to wait but a couple hours. She noticed someone standing at her desk, and looked up. There he was...

"Miss Hargrove, would you have lunch with me today? We have a lot of catching up to do."

"No, thank you, Dr. Parker. I brought my lunch today," she replied.

"Perhaps another day?" he asked.

"Perhaps." she replied, nonchalantly.

He left...

She was not going to make it easy for him, by falling right into his hands like putty. He had hurt her too badly! She seriously doubted if there could ever be anything between them again. The pain was just too great! She would not risk being hurt all over again.

Maybe he would ask out one of the other girls. She was sure any of them would be thrilled to go out with the handsome new doctor. They were all attractive girls, and she could tell from the way they watched him, that they were attracted to him. They tended to swoon every time they saw him. But who was she to tell them what to do. It was their heart he would probably break. She knew him... they didn't! They had no idea of the heartache she'd been through because of this man. She had never told them.

She was glad when it was time to leave work and go home. It had been a long, stressful day. Aunt Pat, bless her dear heart, had supper ready when she arrived home, as she did every night. She still liked to spoil Rachel, who seemed like her own daughter. Rachel didn't mind at all, and loved her like a mother. In fact, she had been with her longer than she had with her real mother, since she was only ten when her parents were killed.

After supper, they took their dessert of chocolate pie, and went to sit on the front porch. It was a warm, peaceful summer evening and just the kind of weather Rachel loved. Just as she was finishing up her pie, and about to relax, she heard the phone ring. She jumped up and ran into the house, to answer it.

"Hargrove residence," she said cheerfully.

"Rachel," and then there was a pause.

"Yes, this is Rachel."

"It's Mitch. Please don't hang up on me."

"What do you want?"

"I need to talk to you," he said.

"About what?" she asked coldly.

He could tell from the tone of her voice that she wasn't happy to hear from him. "Please Rachel... I really do need to see you. Please don't say no... Maybe I could take you to a quiet place for dinner tomorrow night?" he said in the form of a half question.

"I really don't think there is any reason for you to see me. What we had has been over for eight years."

"I know, and I'm sorry. I truly am," he replied.

He sounded sorry, but that didn't make up for all the pain he had put her through. She asked him why he needed to see her.

"I have some things I need to explain to you," he stated. "Please, Rachel... please say yes!"

After a brief pause, she agreed to go with him. She would hear him out. She knew he wouldn't give up, so she might as well get it over with. After all, it would be interesting to see what he had to say for himself.

"I'll pick you up at seven o'clock, if that's okay. I'll need some directions to your house. My memory is a little foggy, after all these years."

"Seven is fine", she said. After giving him directions, they hung up the phone.

She went back out on the porch where Aunt Pat was still waiting for her. She told her about the phone call and her plans to have dinner with Mitch. "Do you think I should go?" she asked.

"Yes, I think you should go and hear him out," said her Aunt.

"I will listen this time and hear what he has to say. I am tired of excuses!"

"I think you will make the right decision, my dear Rachel."

"I hope so," she replied.

She hurried home from work the next evening. She was trying to decide what to wear. She didn't want to over dress, but yet she didn't want to under dress. She finally settled on a lavender flowered skirt, and a matching solid lavender top. No matter what she wore, she always looked beautiful.

At exactly 6:55 p.m., Mitch pulled into her driveway. He got out of his car and walked toward the house. Brownie ran to the screen door and started barking. Nothing escaped her ears and eyes.

"It's okay, Brownie," said Rachel, as she opened the door and invited Mitch in.

"Rachel, you look really beautiful," said Mitch.

"Thank you," said Rachel. "

"Hello, Pat," he said. "It's good to see you again. You're looking well."

"Thanks, and so are you," she answered.

He looked at Rachel and asked, "Are you ready to go? I made dinner reservations for 7:30 p.m." He seemed to be nervous.

"Yes, I'm ready. See you later, Aunt Pat," said Rachel.

"Have a good time," replied Aunt Pat.

Mitch opened the door and followed Rachel outside. When they reached the car, he went around to the passenger side and opened the door for her. She thanked him and got in. He started the car, and drove about ten minutes, to a cozy little French Restaurant, called LE GOURMET CAFE. He parked the car, got out, came around and opened her door. He had been a perfect gentleman so far, she thought.

"Thank you," she said as she slid her long shapely legs out of the car. Her skirt was several inches above her knees, so there was no way of hiding her gorgeous tanned legs.

They walked toward the restaurant at a slow pace. Again, he opened the door and walked in behind her. The maitre de' met them, confirmed their reservation, and showed them to a table for two. Mitch pulled out her chair, then went around and seated himself. He took her hand and gave her a long, lingering look of passion. This made her very uncomfortable. She had to be on the defense... and not let him break her heart again.

A waitress came with menus, and the spell was broken. Since she had never eaten here, she asked Mitch to order for her. It didn't matter what she got, it was going to be hard to eat at all. Being with him, made her nervous, and ill at ease. He just seemed so different from what he used to be. He was a big city doctor, who came back to the country. She wondered if the adjustment would be hard for him. She also wondered why he chose a small town, when he could have stayed in Boston, had a big practice, and worked at a big hospital. There were so many things she wondered about him. She had so many unanswered questions...

The waitress brought the food and after saying the

blessing, they began to eat. She felt like she was going to choke, with each bite she put in her mouth. Finally she choked down most of the food on her plate, and declined dessert. She was sure the food was delicious, but she hardly tasted any of it. She just chewed and swallowed it. Her mind was not on the food.

They sat and talked for an hour. It was mostly small talk. There was one question she had for him, and she needed an answer. She needed to know 'why' he had quit writing and calling her. This had haunted her for the past eight years. She needed to know if it was something she did, or did he find another girlfriend. She finally got up the nerve and asked him.

He looked surprised that she brought up this subject. He was hoping it wouldn't enter into their conversation. Girls don't let things go like guys do. They always need to know the 'why' of everything. He may as well open up and talk about it, as she wasn't going to let it rest.

"I heard you had started dating someone else, so I thought it would be best to set you free. I knew I had eight long years of schooling ahead of me, and it wasn't fair to you to ask you to wait," said Mitch.

"I waited and waited," said Rachel. "I never dated anyone for over a year. I was so crushed that I had lost you, and it took me years to get over you." Here she was telling him the exact thing she said she wouldn't tell him. Somehow, it just slipped out. She wondered who could have told him that she was dating, when it wasn't true. She knew many of the girls in high school were very jealous of her, because she had Mitch. She figured it had to be one of them. Even if it was, they never got him either, since he was still single. I guess all they cared was the fact that she lost him. Their mission was accomplished.

She broke her chain of thought, and continued her conversation with Mitch. "When I saw you Saturday night, all those hurtful feelings came rushing back. All we can ever be is friends. We have no choice since we will be working in the same office."

"But Rachel, it really hurts me to hear you say this. I never stopped loving you for one minute. You've heard the saying... 'If you love something... set it free... If it comes back, it's yours. If it doesn't, it never was yours.' I had to set you free, but I knew in my heart that one day we would be back together. That is the reason I came back to Columbus, to set up my practice. I was praying you wouldn't be married, and I hadn't waited too long. I dated some in college, but there was never anyone who could compare to you. I never even came close to falling in love, because my heart was already full of love for you. Rachel, you are my one True Love... My Soul Mate... and I want to marry you."

She was so stunned by his words, and didn't know what to say. She needed time... he had been gone for eight years, and she had learned to live without him. This was all so new to her. In her heart she knew she still loved him. In fact, she had never stopped loving him.

"Rachel, will you marry me?" asked Mitch. "We have wasted enough time. I want to marry you as soon as possible."

"I don't know what to say!" said Rachel.

"Say yes, please say yes, Rachel. I love you so very much...I always have... I always will."

" Yes, Mitch... I will marry you!" said Rachel. Now, here she had done what she said she wouldn't do. She had fallen right into his hands like putty. "I will need time to plan our wedding. Give me three months to get the details worked out. We will have a small wedding with family and close friends."

"Sounds good to me," said Mitch excitedly. "I can't wait for us to begin our new life together."

"And I can't wait to tell Aunt Pat!" exclaimed Rachel, excitedly. "Can we go now, and tell her our wonderful news?"

"Of course, my dear! How do you think she will react? Will she be upset?"

"I think she will be happy for us, Mitch. She saw how I pined for you for all those years. She kept telling me if it was in God's will for us to be together, He would work it out. She said it would be His time... not ours. Now must be His time, because He has finally worked it out and brought us back together."

Mitch paid the bill and they left the restaurant. Rachel was on Cloud Nine. She sure felt a lot better going out, than she did coming in. She hadn't been this happy since Homecoming night, when they had been crowned King and Queen. That seemed so long ago...They walked to the car holding hands. She felt eighteen again!

The ride home was magical. She felt like Cinderella at the ball. She was on top of the world. After eight years of waiting, she was going to marry the love of her life, the man of her dreams.

Aunt Pat had the front porch light on. Brownie heard the car pull up and was looking out the door. She started barking, as a greeting to her best friend, Rachel. She was always so excited to see her come home.

As soon as they walked in the door, Aunt Pat, who was sitting on the sofa knitting, knew something was up. She could see the happiness in both their faces. Before they even sat down, Rachel blurted out, "Aunt Pat... we're getting married!" Now, Aunt Pat had a huge grin on her face.

"Congratulations, my dears! I knew you two were meant to be together! I am so happy for you! I am very thankful that God worked it all out. So... when's the wedding?"

"In 3 months," replied Mitch. "That's all the time I'm giving her. We've been apart far too long already, and there's no use wasting any more time."

They would both be twenty seven soon. They had discussed having children right away. They wanted to have them while they were still young.

Three months isn't very long to plan a wedding, but Rachel knew she could do it. She would hire a caterer to take care of all the food and wedding cake. That would leave the flowers, photographer, and music for her, and maybe some minor details.

Chapter 7

She and Aunt Pat went to Billings to do their shopping. She found a beautiful sequined Wedding Gown, with a long veil. It was a perfect fit, and didn't need any alterations. For that she was thankful. She looked stunning in it, according to Aunt Pat. Of course, she had to take her Aunt with her, since she had been 'her mother' for the past seventeen years.

They also shopped for Aunt Pat's dress, which was a pale blue two-piece, with lovely lace and sequins.

She asked her best friend Karla, from church, to be her Maid of Honor. Karla happily accepted and said she would be honored. She would be the only attendant Rachel would have.

She would be wearing a beautiful long pale pink dress. Aunt Pat would walk her down the aisle and give her away. She would be honored to have her Aunt by her side.

Mitch was having his older brother Blake, as his Best Man. He had already ordered their tuxedos... to be picked up the day before the ceremony. Things were coming along nicely. He realized that Rachel had much more to do than he did. She was doing most of the work, but that is how girls are, he's been told. They want to be in charge and have things done their way, which was okay with him. He was just happy that she had agreed to marry him.

Finally, the big day was there... Rachel was running around in circles, trying to get last minute things done. The reception would be in the church fellowship hall, and that was one thing she didn't have to worry about. The caterers would take care of everything.

She just wanted to concentrate on making herself look as pretty as possible, to walk down the aisle and marry the man she intended to spend the rest of her life with.

The musicians would be there at 12:30 p.m. They had to get everything set up and ready for the wedding at 2:00 p.m.

The church was already decorated with beautiful roses of different colors. The rose had always been Rachel's favorite flower, and it was hard to choose a color, so she decided to use mixed colors, which was probably even more beautiful than using one color.

Soon, she would be Mrs. Mitch Parker. Somehow she liked the sound of that. With her makeup and hair done professionally, she was a picture of beauty. She put on her wedding gown, with the help of Karla, her Maid of Honor, and was waiting in the church basement. They would come up the steps, into the foyer and listen for the sound of the wedding music. Karla would go in just ahead of her. At the exact right time, she and her dear Aunt Pat would start their walk down the aisle. She was not nervous... she was overjoyed.

Dum Dum De Dum... they started down the aisle. She looked at Aunt Pat, who had the biggest grin on her face. She could tell her aunt was happy for her. Rachel knew she had a big smile on her face, as well. She looked at Mitch, who was looking at her, and they never took their eyes off each other as she made her way down the aisle. How handsome he is, she thought. I am the luckiest girl in the world! She couldn't believe she was marrying the Love of her Life!

Pastor Steve was standing in front of them, Bible in hand, ready to begin the marriage ceremony. Rachel and Mitch had written their own vows, which were very touching... about past, present, and future. After a few words from Pastor Steve, Mitch took Rachel's hand and started his vows...

"Rachel, I fell in love with you the moment I laid eyes on you. We were only seventeen. I knew you were the only woman for me and that one day, I would marry you. I didn't want to leave you, but I had no choice. I had to be able to support you, in the way you deserve to be taken care of. In my heart, I knew I would come back for you and I prayed you would still be single. God answered my prayers and here we are today, about to become one. I love you with all my heart, Rachel. I look forward to our future together... ours and our children."

With tears in her eyes, Rachel started her vows... "Mitch, I have loved you for so long. I never stopped loving you, even when I thought I had lost you forever. You are the love of my life and always have been. I never thought I'd ever be marrying you, but I am so thankful that God gave us a second chance. God has prepared us for each other, and brought us together in His own time. I look forward to spending the rest of my life with you, and the children that God will bless us with. I love you Mitch, now and forever."

There was hardly a dry eye in the church. This wedding was indeed a miracle...

It was a beautiful ceremony! Pastor Steve pronounced them husband and wife, and looking at Mitch, said, "You may now kiss your Bride."

Mitch really took this to heart, and kissed her most passionately. They seemed to float down the aisle to the Wedding March, as they exited the church.

Then it was back in the church to take pictures, before going to the Fellowship Hall for the reception. They cut the cake, and stuffed each other's mouth full, while smearing it on their faces. They were having so much fun! They had made a lot of wonderful memories today.

Four hours later, they were on their way to a glorious two week Honeymoon in Cancun, Mexico. Mitch had previously made reservations at the Hacienda TresRios. This was a Resort, Spa, and Nature Park.

They arrived to find the resort as beautiful as they had hoped. He had rented the Honeymoon suite for them. He had to do it just right. He had this beautiful Angel, and only the BEST was good enough for her.

They had different activities lined up, such as going to the spa, nature tours, and a zip line tour, through the mangrove forests. These were lots of fun. But they mostly wanted to spend time on the beach, relaxing, and just enjoy each other's company. They had so many years of catching up... Mitch never failed to tell Rachel how beautiful she was. He was so blessed that she had given him a second chance. Not everyone is as lucky as he was. He knew that... and was determined never to let himself forget.

This was an unforgettable trip! They took lots of pictures to show family and friends. The time was drawing to a close and it was time to go home. They dreaded leaving the beautiful beaches of Cancun, but nothing lasts forever. Little did they know...

They got up early the morning of departure, had a final breakfast, went to the airport, and boarded a plane home to Montana. They came back with golden tans, sweet memories, lots of pictures and souvenirs.

They were ready to begin their life as husband and wife. They had rented an apartment on Lyle Street, in Columbus, near the office. They would live here until their house was finished. Shortly before Mitch moved to Columbus, he bought a 500 acre ranch in Laurel, Montana. He had hired a contractor to build him a large 2 story log house. He had plans to marry Rachel then, even though she didn't know it. He was hoping and praying that she was still available. God heard his prayer, and after a little persuading, she accepted his proposal. They were meant to be together... they both knew that. She was very happy about the house, as it was in her hometown, where she was born and raised until she was ten, at which time her parents died.

Things were coming along nicely with the house. The men were working at a steady pace, knowing the doctor wanted to move as soon as possible. Mitch was hoping to move in a couple months. Rachel was very excited... Meanwhile she continued to work at the medical clinic, but she would quit her job when they moved. She and Mitch wanted to start a family right away. He thought she should stay home and get plenty of rest. He wanted her not to be stressed when she got pregnant. This would not be good for their baby.

The house was finished in two months, just like the contractor told them. They got everything moved, which wasn't very much. They had to buy all new furniture, which was so much fun for Rachel. She was like a kid in a candy store. Mitch let her pick out anything and everything she wanted. She was the luckiest girl in the world, she kept telling herself!

The Parker Ranch was such a peaceful place... You might hear the sound of a cow bawling, or a dog barking. Brownie loved the farm. She was free to run and play wherever she pleased. But she needed a playmate... So they bought a cattle dog, named Raven. She was lots of help with the cattle, but still found time to play with Brownie. She was well trained, and when she worked... she worked.

Rex Blair was their cattle foreman. He was a local cowboy, who had worked all over the state of Montana. He was a very trusted man and had been with them since the beginning. They left all the decisions concerning cattle and farming, up to him. He hired five local cowboys to help with the hundred head of cattle. There was always something to be done on the ranch. They were branding cattle, repairing fences, putting up hay, growing corn, or exercising the five Arabian horses. Everything ran smoothly most of the time.

On the weekends, Mitch liked to relax on the ranch. He would saddle up his horse, named Butch, and go for a long ride. Sometimes Rachel would go with him, riding her little mare, named Lilly. Often they would take a picnic lunch.

They would find a big tree, spread out their blanket and enjoy the day. This allowed them to spend time together, and relax, too.

Rachel had never ridden a horse until Lilly. Once she got over being nervous, she loved it. Often she would ride in the early morning, after Mitch had gone to work. She loved feeling the morning breeze blowing through her long golden hair. She and Lilly had really bonded in the past few years. It was almost as if they read each other's thoughts.

Every summer she and Mitch would take a nice long vacation. They went to several exotic places. Each time they hoped she would come home pregnant. But for some reason, it never happened. Year after year, they were disappointed. Maybe it was not God's will for them to have a baby. She had finally come to the place where she had accepted it, and said, "Thy will be done, Dear Heavenly Father."

Chapter 8

Back to reality...

But it finally had happened and Mitch would never know. This made her very sad!

Thank God Mitch had taken out a very large life insurance policy after they married. She would be able to finish paying off the house and ranch. There were so many decisions to be made, and she wondered how she would be able to make the right decisions. She had always depended on Mitch and left the final decisions to him. She knew she had to be strong... She had no other family to depend on, except her Aunt Pat, who meant the world to her.

She would have a child to raise, which wouldn't be easy on her own. She knew Aunt Pat would help all she could. She also knew what she had to do though... she had to get a job. She would work for the next several months until the baby was born. After that, she would see...

Laurel was a much bigger town than Columbus, with a populations of over 6,000 people. It should be easier to find a job here. Come Monday morning, she would go to town and start looking for work. Without a college education, she was limited. Most places wouldn't hire anyone without a college degree, unless it was a factory, or Wal-Mart. She didn't want to work either of these places. She would find whatever she could though, and try to be content. She would prefer office work since she was pregnant. She knew she needed to take care of herself, and not do heavy lifting. That disqualified a lot of jobs.

She would keep Rex on as foreman. He did such a great job with the cattle, and they did generate money. She needed that extra income. She knew Rex would do what was best for her and the ranch. She was so blessed to have him. He loved it here, too. He was an older man in his fifties, who had never been married. He'd been a cowboy all his life. It was the life he loved.

Somehow she got through the weekend. She went to church on Sunday, which lifted her spirit. She missed her old church, Rose Baptist, but she and Mitch had settled in quickly at Laurel Baptist. She had made several good friends. Of course, they made her join the choir. When they found out that she sang specials, they scheduled her for once a month. She and Mitch had enjoyed going there, but now it was hard to go back alone. Yesterday was the first time she had been back since his death. It was very hard, but Pastor Wade Harlow preached an uplifting sermon... just what she needed.

She was up bright and early Monday morning. After eating a bite, she took a shower, did her makeup and hair, then got dressed in a classic suit. She was ready to go job hunting.

First she went by the Laurel Medical Center. They had

just recently hired a new receptionist, who was working out well. They told her they were sorry. She went several other places and got similar stories. She wasn't about to give up, because she really needed a job.

She decided to try the real estate offices in town. There were four of them, so maybe she would have better luck there. Perhaps one of them might need a receptionist. She planned to go to all four. First was Starr Real Estate Corporation, who wasn't hiring. Next was Mountain Realty, who gave her the same answer. Third was Laurel Realty, and they weren't hiring either. She was about to get discouraged. She had one more to go... Big Sky Real Estate Company. Before she got out of her car, she bowed her head, and asked God to let this be the one.

She walked in the front door, head held high, and a charming smile on her face. An elderly woman sat at the receptionist desk. She looked up, gave Rachel a pleasant smile, as she said hello, and introduced herself as Mary Adams.

"Good afternoon to you! My name is Rachel Parker. I would like to apply for a job. Is the owner in?"

"Yes, matter of fact, he is," replied Mary. "I will tell him you are here."

Mary got up and slowly walked down the hallway. Shortly, the owner appeared and asked Rachel to come into his office. She had a good feeling about this place. At least she was getting to talk to the owner. He introduced himself as Bryan Adams, and asked her to take a seat. He looked to be middle aged and seemed very nice. She was feeling better all the time.

After a short interview, he told her this was her lucky

day... that he was indeed looking for a new receptionist. His mother had been filling in for him, until he could hire a new girl. The other one had gotten married and moved away. He asked her if she could start work tomorrow and she quickly told him she could. She was really looking forward to starting her new job.

She shook his hand and thanked him. She told him she really appreciated him taking time to interview her. She told him she would see him in the morning. She left and headed toward her car. She got in and bowed her head..."Thank you, Dear God, for giving me this job. I promise I will do my best. I give you all the honor and glory. In Jesus name I pray...Amen!"

She started her car and headed for the ranch. Her spirit was really lifted and Lord knows she needed that, after all she had been through. The drive home was a good one. Traffic wasn't bad and everything went smoothly. Brownie met her at the door, excited as always.

She slipped out of her suit and into a pair of jeans and a T-shirt. She was most comfortable when she was dressed this way. She fixed herself a ham sandwich, bowl of fruit and a glass of milk. She had to start eating better since she was having a baby. For some reason she really felt hungry. She seemed to be getting her appetite back, which was good, since she was eating for two now.

She had been so busy lately, she'd hardly had time to think about her pregnancy. Everything she did from now on, would be about the baby. She needed to find a new doctor in Laurel, since that is where she would be delivering. She would look in the phone book tomorrow at work, and see who she could find.

Tuesday morning came and it was off to work again. Later in the morning, she found the phone book and looked for the physician section. She found it quickly, then scanned down to the OB/GYN doctors. There were three of them. Since she didn't know any of them, she just chose one... Dr. Nathan Roberts. She dialed the number and heard a pleasant voice on the other end of the line. The receptionist referred her to a nurse, who made an appointment for her on the following Friday at 4:00 p.m. She thanked her and hung up.

She would have to ask off work early, but didn't think that would be a problem. Her boss knew that she recently lost her husband, and was very sympathetic to her. She hadn't told him she was pregnant, but now she would have to. She would do that before she left work today. She hoped that wouldn't cause her to lose her job. She really needed to keep her job. She really hoped he would understand.

A few minutes before 5:00 p.m., Rachel knocked on Mr. Adams' door. He told her to come in. She explained everything to him. He could see fear in her eyes. He told her not to worry that she was in no danger of losing her job. He told her to take off any time she needed to go to the doctor. She felt like hugging his neck, but of course she didn't. She thanked him sincerely, and left.

Friday came and Rachel went for her first visit with Dr. Roberts. The receptionist was very nice and gave her papers to fill out, since this was her first visit. At 4:10 p.m., she was called in to see the doctor. He introduced himself, and, asked her some questions. Then came the dreaded part... the examination. He told her that everything looked fine, and she should have a normal pregnancy and delivery. This made her very happy and relieved. She was 3 months now, and was already on pre-natal vitamins, from her visit to the other doctor in Columbus. Dr. Roberts gave her some exercises to do, which would make delivery easier.

Day after day, she went to work. She loved her new job! Her stomach began to get bigger each day. Her jeans were getting tight, as well as her work clothes. She would soon be in maternity wear. That was exciting!

At five months, they did a sonogram and told her she was having a baby girl. She was so excited! She wondered if Mitch would have been disappointed, since he had his heart set on a son. She couldn't wait to tell Aunt Pat, who was also hoping for a girl. Rachel always went to visit her at least twice a month. She still missed her dear sweet aunt, even though she and Mitch moved away five years ago. God works in mysterious ways. We don't always understand, but he never makes a mistake. He took Mitch, but He's giving her a new daughter, to share her life with.

The next four months went by quickly. She was just a few days away from her due date. She was feeling tired these days, as she had gained twenty five pounds. She was thinking the baby would be big. At least she had taken care of herself and had eaten well, trying to make a healthy baby. She had the nursery ready, with the help of Aunt Pat, who enjoyed it just as much as she did. Baby clothes, diapers, and all necessities had been bought.

The girls at the real estate office gave her a surprise baby shower. It was a joyous occasion. They gave her so many nice things for the baby, including a high chair and a swing. Everyone had been so good to her. She was so thankful for her friends.

The girls from her old office, where Mitch had worked, also gave her a baby shower. That was a nice surprise. They gave her lots of nice things, including a stroller and a car seat. As far as she knew, she had everything she needed... but the baby.

At 2:00 a.m., two days before her due date, she woke up with pains in her back. She got up and walked around some to see if they stopped or got worse. They never stopped... and in about an hour, her water broke. She knew it was time to go to the hospital. She called Aunt Pat, who was there in thirty minutes. She also called Dr. Roberts, and woke him up. He was used to that, so he didn't mind. She got her suitcase, which was already packed, got in the car and headed for Laurel Memorial Hospital, with Aunt Pat driving.

It was a twenty minute drive to the hospital. Aunt Pat went to the Emergency Room parking lot and pulled in a parking space. She helped Rachel out, then grabbed the suitcase, and proceeded toward the Emergency Room door. A nurse met them with a wheelchair, seated Rachel and away they went. Aunt Pat followed them to the waiting room. She had decided she didn't want to be in the delivery room when the baby was born. She was content to wait. If Mitch was alive, Rachel knew he would have wanted to go in with her. She tried not to dwell on that. He was gone... and she would soon have a new baby.

After ten hours of hard labor, little Jennifer Rose Parker, made her entrance into this world. She cried as soon as she was born. The nurse laid her on Rachel's stomach before they even cut the umbilical cord. Rachel fell in love with her that very instant! She was a beautiful little baby girl with a round face, and a head full of black hair, like her daddy.

The nurse cleaned her up, weighed her, and got her dressed. Then she took her to the nursery with all the other babies. Later, when Rachel was back in her room, they brought little Jenny to her. She was even more beautiful after being cleaned up. Rachel looked at the little bracelet on her arm, and saw that she weighed 8 lbs. 2 oz. and was 20 inches long. She was a big baby!

Rachel never imagined she could feel so much love for a baby. It was indescribable... It was a feeling unlike any she had ever had before. You had to experience it, before you could know exactly how it felt. She was so thankful to God for giving her this baby. She would always have a part of Mitch with her, as a reminder of the love they shared.

Aunt Pat came to her room, and got to hold baby Jenny. She was so excited, and you would have thought the baby was hers. Rachel had a feeling that Aunt Pat would be making extra trips to the ranch. She was very happy that she still had her aunt, and that she could be a part of this special occasion.

Rachel spent two days in the hospital and came home the third morning. Aunt Pat had driven them home. She planned to stay a couple weeks and help out. She knew Rachel would need to rest, and build her strength back up. Although, she had never had a baby, she had heard it takes a lot out of a woman. She was going to see that Rachel regained her strength, and was able to take care of little Jenny, before she left and went back to her home.

Rachel was so appreciative that Aunt Pat felt that way. She was going to ask her if she would consider babysitting little Jenny, after she went back to work. She didn't want to go back, but she felt she had no choice.

Rachel finally approached the subject. Aunt Pat was thrilled that she had been asked to care for the baby. She would come over on Sunday nights, and stay until Friday evenings. Then she would go back home for the weekend. That would allow her to attend her own church, and would give Rachel and Jenny time alone.

Rachel was so pleased that Aunt Pat would be caring for Jenny. She didn't like the idea of leaving her with a stranger. This would be good for all of them. Rachel could go to work, and not have to worry about Jenny. She planned to go back when Jenny was two months old. She was breast feeding and would pump enough milk each night, for the following day. Of course, she would have formula and bottles for a standby.

Jenny was a good baby. She hardly cried, except when she was hungry, or needed a clean diaper. That was a blessing... Rachel had heard some mother's talk about having babies with colic. Thank God, Jenny didn't have it. God had really blessed her in so many ways.

Jenny was growing and doing so well. It would soon be her first birthday. Where had the time gone? It seemed like only yesterday, that she had brought her home from the hospital. Of course, she would have to give Jenny a birthday party. So she and Aunt Pat starting making plans for that. It was so much fun having a baby in the house. It didn't seem cold and empty now. Each day brought a new challenge.

Jenny was learning so many new things. Oh how Rachel wished Mitch was here to experience all this with her. Jenny would have been the light of his life!

Work was going well at the real estate office. She had made new friends, with the agents and their families. Jeff had a lovely wife, and two little daughters, Kim and Kasey. She would invite them to Jenny's party. Dale had a pretty young wife, and a two year old son, Danny. That would be another one to invite. Riley was divorced, but had a son, Ryan and daughter, Robin. She would invite them also. That would be six, including Jenny, so she thought that would be enough for a one year old. The oldest was only three, so she would have her hands full. She was sure their mother's would stay at the party also.

Her best friend at work was Taylor, who was also a real estate agent. She was engaged to be married to a very nice guy, named Bill. She had asked Rachel to be her Maid of Honor, which she gladly accepted. Rachel was a stickler for love... She'd had the love of her life, and if she never loved again, that was okay. She and Mitch had more love in those short five years, than most people have in a lifetime. Now, she had Jenny... She had built her life around her beautiful small daughter, who was looking more like her daddy, the older she got. Rachel was happy for that... it somehow made her feel closer to Mitch.

The day of Jenny's birthday party was a beautiful, warm day. This was unusual for March. The sun was shining brightly and not a cloud in the sky. Everything was prepared, and it was almost 12:30. She thought she would have the party at this time, so all the children could go home and take a nap later.

One by one, cars pulled in her driveway. She was excited, but Jenny was too young to know what was going on. All five of the children came, along with their mothers. It was a good, but loud party. One of the six children was crying most of the time. It seems they took turns, Jenny included. The party ended an hour later, and everyone left. Now it was clean-up time. First, she put Jenny down for a nap, then it was back to the kitchen, where Aunt Pat had already started the cleaning process. With both of them working, it didn't take long to get everything back in order.

They retired to the family room, with a cup of coffee. They needed to let their nerves settle. Aunt Pat stayed for another hour, then left for home. She had to get ready for church in the morning.

Chapter 9

The next big event was Taylor's wedding. Rachel was excited for her. She was sure she had found a great guy, who would make her very happy.

Taylor had already bought her wedding gown. It was so beautiful. She had invited Rachel to her house, one day on their lunch break, and she "modeled" it for her. She surely was going to make a beautiful bride. She was a very pretty girl, with long black hair, and dark brown eyes. She was about the same height as Rachel and just as slim.

The next Saturday, Rachel and Taylor went shopping for the maid of honor and bridesmaid dresses. Taylor was using lavender as her color scheme. So she wanted all the girls in lavender. They went to several shops in Billings, before finding the perfect dresses, for her and the two bridesmaids, Vanessa and Nicole. Hers was the same color, but styled a little differently. Rachel tried it on, in a size six, and it was a perfect fit. She looked so glamorous.

Since Taylor's fiancee Bill, didn't have a brother or a father, he was having his old college roommate as his best man. His name was Grayson Sterling. He was from Billings, Montana. They had kept in touch and been friends for many years. His groomsmen were a couple of his cousins, Michael and Hank.

Finally the big day arrived for Taylor and Bill. They were having an outdoor wedding at Lake Elmo, which was a 64 acre reservoir, popular for swimming, boardsailing, non-motorized boating and fishing. The park was 183 acres in size at an elevation of 3,199 feet. It was the perfect place for a wedding. Taylor had always wanted to get married on the beach. This one was close home, so would be convenient for all her family and friends.

The girls and guys all went to the changing rooms and changed into their wedding attire. The moment had come... The band was all set up, and had started playing the music. What a great day this is, thought Rachel. Then she thought of her own wedding, and how happy and excited she and Mitch had been. Then her mind wandered to Jenny, who was home with Aunt Pat. Thank God she didn't have to worry about her. She knew she was in good hands, as long as she was with Aunt Pat.

They formed a line, in the order they would walk down the beach. The girls were wearing no shoes. You couldn't tell it, since they had on long dresses. It would be good to feel the sand between her toes, thought Rachel. It had been too long. She missed the nice vacations that she and Mitch used to take. Now she couldn't afford to take a vacation at all.

The wedding music started and the bridesmaids walked down the white runner, one after another, taking their positions. Then it was Rachel's time to go. She walked slowly... enjoying the sand between her toes, with her mind wandering. When she got to her position, she focused on what she was supposed to be doing. She looked at Bill, then at his best man, Grayson. Her eyes stopped there. She had never seen such a handsome man in all her life! He was very tall, slim, with an olive complexion, and had black wavy hair. He had the most piercing blue eyes she had ever seen in her life. He was staring at her, too! Their eyes had met and held... She could feel her face getting warm, as she made herself look away. What's wrong with me, she asked herself. I shouldn't be looking at another man like that. I still have my loyalty to Mitch. Then another voice within her seemed to say... but Mitch is dead, and he is not coming back, no matter how long you wait. It's time you pick up the pieces and move on.

Rachel jerked her head from his direction. She needed to forget him and concentrate on the wedding. She felt guilty for staring at this hunk of a man.

The preacher performed the ceremony, and pronounced them husband and wife. The wedding was over... and it was time to walk up the white runner, away from the beach. The bride and groom walked as people were throwing bird seeds at them. The bridesmaids & groomsmen walked next... two by two. Then it was her turn to walk with the best man. She was nervous...Grayson walked toward her and she felt her knees get weak. She was glad she was wearing a long dress, or he might have seen her legs trembling.

"Ready to go?" he asked her.

"Yes," she replied.

Somehow the walk seemed to take forever. When they got to the end, he looked at her and said, " My name is Grayson Sterling. I am a long time friend and college roommate of Bill."

"I'm Rachel Parker, and I work with Taylor at Big Sky Real Estate Company, in Laurel."

"I've met several of Taylor's friends. Why haven't I seen you before?"

"I've only known her about one and a half years."

"That explains it. I haven't seen them for over two years," said Grayson.

"Are you married?" asked Grayson.

"No," replied Rachel. "I was married for five years, and my husband was killed in a car accident, over two years ago."

"I am so sorry! I had no idea. I wouldn't have asked if I had known."

"That's okay... You had no way of knowing."

The reception was held in a large picnic shelter near the lake. They had decorated it with lavender flowers, balloons and streamers. It looked beautiful! A buffet bar was set up in the center. Everyone started making their way toward the food.

"Mind if I walk with you?" asked Grayson.

"Not at all," Rachel responded.

They walked in silence the short distance to the buffet bar. Rachel felt good... she felt alive for the first time in over two years.

They got in line, fixed a plate and joined the Bride and Groom at their table. The bridesmaids and groomsmen joined them also. Rachel was glad she didn't have to be alone with him. She really liked him, but she was a little nervous. She hadn't dated anyone since Mitch died, and she felt uncomfortable with herself, for the feelings she was having. Today would soon be over and she probably would never see him again.

"How's things at work Grayson?" asked Bill.

Grayson worked for the U.S. Geological Service in Billings, Montana. He had been with them ever since he graduated from college.

"Glacier National Park has lost two more of its namesake moving icefields to climate change, which is shrinking the rivers of ice until they grind to a halt. Fewer glaciers means less water in streams for the fish and a higher risk for forest fires," said Grayson.

"Mmmmm, not good," said Bill.

"The weather records indicate the Glacier is 2 degrees hotter on average now, compared with 1950 to 1979," said Grayson.

"Enough shop talk," chided Taylor.

"I agree," said Grayson. "So... where are you going on your Honeymoon?"

"To Cancun, Mexico," replied Taylor.

"For how long?" asked Grayson.

"Two glorious weeks," said Taylor excitedly.

"Have fun, and be safe," said Grayson.

"Thanks, we will," she responded.

Everyone was finished eating and waiting for the Bride and Groom to cut the cake. It was a beautiful 3 tier wedding cake, with lots of lavender roses on each layer. It sure took a lot of talent to make a cake this perfect. There were people who could do it, but Rachel was not one of them. She did well to bake a cake and put on plain icing. She was not a fancy cook.

With both hands on the knife, together they cut the cake. Taylor picked up the first piece and stuffed it in Bill's mouth. Of course she made sure it went all over his face. Now it was his turn... They cut another piece, which he picked up and crammed into her mouth. He was nicer to her though... he didn't smear it all over her face, as badly as she did on his. Then he leaned over and kissed her long and hard. She was surprised!

Now it was time for the rest of them to have a piece of wedding cake. It was as delicious as it looked.

Then it was time to leave. Grayson turned to her and said, "It was very nice to meet you Rachel. Maybe we'll meet again one day."

"Nice to meet you, too. Perhaps our paths will cross again someday."

He walked her to her car, opened the door for her, and she got in. After a polite goodbye, he left, and headed to his car.

Chapter 10

She started her car and headed home to the ranch. This had been a good day. She was happy she could be a part of her best friend's wedding. She truly hoped that Taylor and Bill would be as happy as she and Mitch had been those short five years. She prayed Taylor would never know the pain of losing her husband. She wouldn't wish that on anyone.

Jenny was having her supper when Rachel walked in the door. Aunt Pat was feeding her mixed vegetables from a baby food jar. Jenny looked, saw her mommy and spread her mouth into a big grin. The mixed vegetables were running down her chin. She was too excited to eat. Rachel walked over and kissed her on the top of the head. She loved this little girl so much!

She left Aunt Pat to finish feeding Jenny, while she changed out of her weeding attire. She put on a pair of jeans and a T-shirt. This felt much better. She had been in high heels all day, and it was such a relief to pull those off. Now she could relax and reflect over the day.

Later she bathed Jenny and put her to bed. She asked

Aunt Pat if she would like to go sit on the front porch and hear about her day. She hardly knew where to start. Of course, Aunt Pat was all ears.

"I never thought I would be saying this, but I met the most amazing, handsome man today. His name is Grayson Sterling, and he was Bill's best man. They went to college together. We sat together at the reception and you know, it actually felt good to be able to talk to a man."

"Well, good for you, Rachel."

"As much as I enjoyed it, I kind of felt guilty though. I felt like I was betraying Mitch."

"Girl... you have to get over that! It's time you move on. I know you loved Mitch with all your heart, but he's gone. You can't keep living in the past."

"Oh well, I probably will never see him again anyway. He lives in Billings and works for the U.S. Geological Service. He travels a lot."

"Just like I told you before, Rachel... If it's meant to be, God will work everything out. I truly believe that."

" I know. I believe that, too. But sometimes it is hard for me."

The weekend was over and it was back to work on Monday. Things were going smoothly at work. Jeff, her divorced co-worker had asked her out to dinner this coming Friday night. They had become good friends. She knew he liked her, but on her part, knew they would never be anything more than friends. She didn't want to hurt him by leading him on. They were just two friends having dinner together.

Jeff picked her up at 6:30 p.m. He came in the house and met Aunt Pat, who was staying over to babysit. After a brief conversation, they left. He took her to the local Mexican Restaurant. He was a perfect gentleman. They talked for awhile, after they finished eating, and then he took her home. He walked her to the door.

"I had a good time. Thanks for going out with me," said Jeff.

"Thanks for asking me, and thanks for dinner. I had a good time, too."

He gave her a friendly hug, said goodnight and walked to his car.

Rachel went into the house. Aunt Pat had already put Jenny to bed, so they had time to talk and reflect her true feelings about this evening.

"How did things go," asked her aunt.

"We had a good time," said Rachel, "but there was no 'love' connection. He's just a good friend. I'm not so sure that he wouldn't like it to be more, but in my heart I know he is not the one for me. If I ever marry again, I have to be certain he is the 'right' one. I probably won't go out with him again. I don't want to lead him on. He is too nice to be hurt. I hope he can find true love again. I just know it's not me."

"You speak with wisdom, my dear," said her aunt. "I am very proud of you for not leading this man on, then breaking his heart."

This was Rachel's first date since Mitch died. She wasn't sure she was ready to date. She doubted if she would ever fall in love again.

Time passed... Jenny turned two years old. Rachel gave her another party, and invited the same children as before. Jenny really enjoyed her party this time. She laughed and squealed and smeared cake all over her face. This made really cute pictures. It sure was hard to believe she was two.

Her friend Taylor, had just found out she was pregnant. She and Bill were overjoyed. Their marriage was going really well, and Taylor seemed to be very happy. This made Rachel happy, for her.

"Don't give up Rachel," Taylor told her. "You'll find true love again. I promise."

Rachel wanted to believe her, but wasn't sure it would ever happen to her again.

"By the way," said Taylor. "Bill called Grayson last night to tell him about the baby. Grayson was asking about you. I thought you'd like to know."

"What did he ask about me?" asked Rachel.

"He wanted to know if you had remarried yet. When Bill told him no, he asked if you were dating anyone."

"What did Bill tell him?" asked Rachel.

"He told him you were waiting on him," said Taylor.

"He didn't!!" exclaimed Rachel.

"He did!" said Taylor laughing.

"What did Grayson say?" asked Rachel.

"He said he needs to make a trip to Laurel."

"Oh, my goodness...Did he say when he is coming?" asked Rachel

"He's coming next weekend," said Taylor. "He's out of town this week. He said he is going to call you when he gets here on Friday night. He's going to ask you out, Rachel."

"I don't know what to say," replied Rachel, with a big smile.

"Say 'YES'... don't turn him down. You know you're attracted to him."

"I have to admit it... I am! He's the first man I've met since Mitch, that I feel I could possibly have a relationship with."

"I'm glad to hear you say that, Rachel. Grayson is a super guy. He's never been married... always said he was waiting for the right girl," said Taylor.

"And you think I might be the 'right' girl for him?" she asked.

"You very well could be. Look at you! What man wouldn't fall in love with you?"

"I guess I never thought of myself in that way," said Rachel.

"I think Grayson is ready to settle down. He's thirty five years old, and he'd like to marry and have a family before he gets much older."

"I can understand that," said Rachel.

"I have to run now... I've got to show a house in half an hour. We'll talk later."

The next week went by slowly. All she could think about was Grayson coming on Friday. She hoped he would call, as he had told Bill. She hoped he wanted to go out with her as much as she wanted to go out with him. She hoped he wouldn't let her down. Only time would tell... She was beginning to feel like a school girl again. She hadn't felt this young and alive for so long.

Friday finally came. She left work at 5:00 p.m. as usual. She was feeling good! She arrived home, to find Jenny in a good mood. She came right to her mommy and hugged her neck so tight. This always melted Rachel's heart. She was such a precious, sweet, little girl.

Aunt Pat was so happy to see Rachel feeling better and not pining so much. It was time she lived a little. She was more than happy to babysit, so Rachel could go out and 'live' again.

After supper, and the dishes were washed, they took Jenny and went to the front porch. Jenny loved to go outside. She had a swing in the front yard, which she loved. Rachel pushed her in it, and she was full of giggles. Aunt Pat sat on the porch watching them, with a warm feeling in her heart. She loved her two 'girls' so much.

Chapter 11

Just then the phone rang. Aunt Pat went to answer it. She came back and told Rachel it was for her. A big smile crossed Rachel's face. "Who is it?" she asked.

"He said his name was Grayson." said her aunt.

Even a bigger smile graced her face. Aunt Pat went to swing Jenny, while Rachel took the phone call.

"Hello Grayson," said Rachel with a perky voice.

"Hi Rachel. It sure is good to hear your voice again." said Grayson.

"Thanks, and you, too," said Rachel.

"I guess Taylor told you I would be calling. " he stated.

"Yes she did. She was so excited to get to tell me."

"Did she tell you what I wanted?" he asked.

" Not sure... but she did say something about you asking me out." said Rachel, feeling a little embarrassed.

"That is exactly why I called. That is the only reason I came to Laurel this weekend. I had to see you again. I haven't been able to get you off my mind."

Rachel hardly knew what to say. She really wanted to see

him again, but just couldn't tell him. She had to take it slowly. She didn't want to rush into anything.

"Will you go out to dinner with me tomorrow night?" he asked.

"Thank you for asking, and I will be delighted to go out with you," she said.

"I will pick you up at 6:00 p.m., if that's okay with you. I need directions to your house, too."

Rachel told him that 6:00 p.m. would be fine, then she gave him directions to her ranch. She had about 22 hours to think about what to wear. She wanted everything to be just perfect.

She went back outside with the biggest grin on her face ever. Aunt Pat was smiling, too. She could tell from the look on Rachel's face, that everything went well in her conversation with Grayson. Seeing Rachel happy, made her happy. After all, this was her family.

Saturday came, and Rachel had decisions to make. She wanted to look her best for Grayson, but not dress up too much. After all, she had no idea where he was taking her to eat.

Later that afternoon, she did her hair and makeup. About thirty minutes before time for Grayson to arrive, she slipped into a beautiful pale green dress, that matched her eyes. She had shoes to match. She loved wearing green, as it always enhanced her beautiful green eyes.

A few minutes before 6:00 p.m., she saw a silver BMW pull into her driveway. She knew it had to be him. He parked, got out and came up the front steps. Brownie met him at the door, barking her hello greeting to him. He talked a few minutes to Brownie, who stopped barking and started wagging her tail. Rachel went to the door, and invited him in. She couldn't wait to introduce him to Aunt Pat and Jenny.

"Grayson, this is my Aunt Pat and my daughter Jenny," she said.

"Nice to meet you Aunt Pat," he said, as he kissed her hand. "Nice to meet you to, Jenny," he said, as he kissed her on the cheek. Jenny looked at him so strangely, but never cried. Instead, she gave him a big smile.

"You're a beautiful little girl, Jenny," he exclaimed. "How old are you?"

"Thank you, and she is two years old."

"I guess we had better go, since I made reservations for 6:30 p.m."

They said their goodbyes to Aunt Pat and Jenny, and walked out the door and he said, "By the way, you look absolutely beautiful tonight, Rachel."

"Thank you, Grayson," she replied with a lovely smile. "You look very nice also."

"Thanks, Rachel."

He opened the car door and she sat down. He went around to the driver's side and got in. He couldn't believe he had this beautiful woman in his car. What a blessing from God!

Rachel was thinking about the same thing. She knew that God had a hand in them meeting. There was no other explanation.

They drove about twenty minutes and finally came to the Tuscan, an Italian Restaurant. He parked the car near the entrance, got out, came around and opened her door.

She got out and thanked him. They walked to the entrance of the restaurant. He held the door open for her and walked in behind her. He was a true gentleman. They were shown to a table right away. He seated her, then seated himself beside her.

"I'm glad you decided to come to dinner with me tonight," said Grayson.

"I'm glad you asked me," she said smiling.

"It's my pleasure. You are a beautiful woman, Rachel."

"Thank you," she replied.

The waitress came with menus. After a few minutes, they both decided on pasta. She took their orders, and left. They talked while waiting for their food.

"There's so much I want to know about you, Rachel. Tell me about your young life, and growing up."

"I hardly know where to begin. I was born and raised in Laurel, until I was ten years old. My parents were killed in a horrible car accident. I went to live with my dad's only sister, Pat Hargrove, in Columbus. I graduated from high school, but never went to college. After my parent's bills were paid, there was no money left. I didn't care because I felt like I needed to get a job and help Aunt Pat. After all, she had made a lot of sacrifices for me. I felt like I owed her, even though she said I didn't. She has never been married, so she took me in and raised me like I was her own daughter. I was so blessed to have her. I don't know what would have happened to me, if it wasn't for her. She has always been there for me, no matter what the situation was. I owe her so much."

"You were lucky to have her," said Grayson.

"Don't I know? I have been so blessed to have her in my

life. She was there for me when I married Mitch, and again when he died. She was all I had. Without her, I couldn't have made it."

"How did you meet Mitch?" he asked.

"We were high school sweethearts. He went off to college to be a doctor, and our relationship ended. After high school, I went to work for the Columbus Medical Clinic. In later years, Mitch came back and went to work there. It was such a shock to see him. The rest is history."

"What about your baby? Was she born before or after your husband died?"

"After. I was only two months pregnant when he got killed. He didn't even know I was pregnant. I had cooked a special dinner for him, and was going to tell him that night, but he never made it home. I have felt so guilty that I never told him before he died."

"I am so sorry, Rachel!" he said with sympathy.

"We had five wonderful years together, and he gave me my precious baby daughter. I feel so blessed to have her."

"And you should. Children are a gift from God," he said.

"What about you? Tell me about yourself, " said Rachel.

"There's not a lot to tell. You already know I went to college and work for the U.S. Geological Service in Billings. I also grew up in Billings, with an older brother, Tyler and younger sister, Hannah. They are both married, with two children each. My parents have been married for almost forty five years. I know I am blessed to still have them. All my family lives in Billings. It is nice to have everyone close.

We get together as often as we can. With my travels, it is not always possible for me to be there. I am hoping for a promotion soon, and if I get it, I won't be traveling much at all. I am ready to slow down... I would like to have a family before I get too old," he said with a laugh.

"Have you ever been married?" she asked. She knew Taylor told her he hadn't been, but she wanted to hear what he had to say.

"Nope, I never found the right girl. I wasn't about to 'settle' just to get married. I think you need to make sure you have the right one before rushing into marriage."

"I couldn't agree with you more," she said.

"This has been really nice tonight. I look forward to seeing you again soon, and getting to know you better."

"I would like that, too.

He paid the check and they left. He drove slowly to her house, as if he didn't want this night to end. She was on cloud nine. She remembered feeling that way, once before. She never thought she would ever find true love again. But she was beginning to think she had found it.

He walked her to the door, gave her a tight hug, and a brief kiss on the check. He told her he would call her soon. She was hoping he would. She would eagerly wait for his call.

She watched him drive away, before entering the house. Of course, Aunt Pat was waiting to hear all the details. She lived her life through Rachel. Rachel had so much to tell her. She was so happy to see her little girl coming alive again.

Chapter 12

They sat and talked for two hours. Aunt Pat knew that Rachel had found her true love for the second time. She had often told her, that you have to open up your heart and take a risk. If you don't, you will be alone for the rest of your life. Tonight she felt that Rachel had listened to her, and opened up her heart to love. She was very happy for her. It made her mind wander back to the days long ago, when she was so much in love with Roman Hunter. He had left her standing at the altar. In all these years, she had never heard a word from him, or even about him. He seemed to have dropped off the face of the earth.

She should have taken her own advice and looked for someone else, but she didn't. She told herself she was destined to be alone the rest of her life. Now she was living her life through Rachel. That was okay... she had gotten used to being alone.

Grayson called Rachel the following weekend, and asked her if she was free on Saturday night. If so, he would drive over to Laurel on Friday night.

"I haven't made any plans, and yes, I would love to see you again," she said excitedly.

"I have been thinking...how would you like to go on a picnic Saturday around noon, and take your Aunt Pat and your daughter Jenny?"

"That sounds wonderful," Rachel said.

"I will bring the food," he stated.

"Let me talk to Aunt Pat and get her input first," said Rachel.

"I will wait while you go ask her."

Rachel went to talk to Aunt Pat, who was thrilled at the thought of a picnic. It had been so long since they had been on one. She spoke up and said, "Tell Grayson, I will fix all the food." She knew her food would be much better than any he could buy.

"Are you sure?" asked Rachel.

"Of course, dear. I wouldn't have it any other way," she responded.

Rachel went back to the phone. "Aunt Pat insists that she will fix all the food. You may as well let her have her own way."

"Whatever makes her happy, is fine with me," said Grayson.

"We have many lovely places on the ranch for a picnic. Unless you have something in mind, we could do it here."

"Oh... of course, that will be fine with me."

"Great... then everything is settled and we'll look for you next Saturday around noon."

"I'll be there, and I can't wait to see you again."

"Me too," she said, trying to keep the excitement out of her voice.

They hung up the phone and she went to talk to Aunt Pat, about her menu. She knew her aunt would outdo herself, just to show Grayson what a great cook she was. That was okay.

The week went by slowly as she anticipated another date with Grayson. She was really beginning to like this man a lot. She didn't feel guilty anymore. She was glad she had finally gotten over those feelings. Now she felt like Mitch would want her to go on with her life, and find someone to love her and Jenny.

Saturday finally came and Aunt Pat was busy as a beaver, working in the kitchen preparing food for the picnic. She was doing something that she really loved. She was a wonderful cook, and loved to be told that.

Grayson pulled in the driveway shortly before noon. Aunt Pat was doing the finishing touches and packing the food in a huge picnic basket. She must be planning on them eating a lot. One thing about her, she loved to see people eat her food. She sure would have made a wonderful wife for some man. Oh well, it's Roman's loss!

Grayson knocked on the door, and Rachel answered it, with Jenny in her arms. Grayson spoke and reached out his arms to Jenny. Surprisingly, she went to him. Usually she doesn't take up with strangers that fast, especially men. Rachel could see that he was surprised also.

Soon they were ready and headed out the door. It was a beautiful, warm day and the sun was shining brightly. It was a perfect day for a picnic. Rachel had a jeep, which she used when she wanted to ride over the ranch. They all climbed into it, with Rachel in the driver's seat. They went about a mile, until they came to a beautiful area with several big shade trees, nestled along a babbling brook. This was a perfect place for a picnic. The only sounds were the brook, and some birds singing in the trees. It was so peaceful!

They spread out the blanket, and placed the picnic basket in the middle. They all sat down, and Aunt Pat opened up the basket. There was a wonderful aroma coming from within. She began to remove the food, which consisted of Fried Chicken, Potato Salad, Macaroni Salad, Baked Beans, Rolls and Fried Apple Pies. Grayson looked at the food, and you could almost see his mouth watering. He wasn't used to this kind of country cooking. He couldn't wait to get started eating. First, Aunt Pat said the blessing, and they all began to dig in.

"This is wonderful!" exclaimed Grayson. "You are a great cook, Aunt Pat. It is amazing that some man hasn't already snapped you up."

A clouded look came on her face. At once he knew he had said the wrong thing. He looked at Rachel, and she kind of shook her head. He knew not to say anything more. Rachel would tell him sometime, when Aunt Pat wasn't around.

They all ate until they were full. Jenny had eaten, then fell asleep on the blanket. They packed up the food that was left, and set the basket under a big shade tree. Aunt Pat told Rachel to take Grayson for a walk and she would stay with Jenny.

"Good idea," said Rachel. "Thank you!"

" Want to go for a walk, Grayson?" she asked.

"Sure. I need to walk off some of this great lunch that I just ate."

Grayson took her hand and they walked over to the edge of the brook. The water was running swiftly over the rocks, making a babbling sound. This was Heaven on earth! It was such a peaceful place to be.

"Would you like to sit here and talk awhile?" asked Grayson.

"That would be nice," replied Rachel.

So they sat down and started to talk. Not long into their conversation, Grayson suddenly said, "Rachel, I have something to tell you and I hope it's not too soon... I have fallen in love with you!"

She was caught off guard... but somehow she wasn't surprised either, as she could see it in his eyes. "That makes me very happy, Grayson. I am in love with you, too! I never thought I would ever fall in love again..."

With a big grin, he replied, "Well, that's wonderful! I wasn't sure how you would react. I don't want to rush you, but I had to tell you how I feel," he said.

"I'm glad you told me!"

"I didn't want to risk losing you to someone else, by hiding my feelings for too long. You are a very beautiful young woman, and I know many men would love to marry you. I'm glad I got here in time. I was attracted to you from the first time I saw you at Bill and Taylor's wedding. I think I knew that day, that you were the woman I would marry one day."

"Since you're confessing, I will too!" said Rachel. "The

first time I looked into those piercing blue eyes of yours, that did me in."

"Really?" asked Grayson, smiling.

"Yes!" exclaimed Rachel. "You have the most beautiful eyes I've ever seen. It's as if they are piercing my soul, and can see all the secrets of my heart."

"That's good," he said, staring at her with eyes full of love. "What are my eyes seeing now?"

"They're seeing the love for you, in my heart."

Rachel looked over to where Jenny was sleeping, and saw that she was awake, and playing with Aunt Pat. They seemed to be having such a good time.

"I guess we had better get back to reality, and see what the two of them are doing," she said, pointing to her aunt and daughter.

They walked back over there, and Rachel picked up her daughter, while Grayson and Aunt Pat folded the blanket. He picked up the picnic basket and headed to the jeep. They loaded the supplies, got in and headed back to the ranch. It had been a most wonderful day!

Chapter 13

Grayson had to leave soon and go back to Billings. Aunt Pat left shortly afterward. It had been a great day for her, but she had no way of knowing how things would even get better once she got back home. For now, she was thinking of Rachel, and it did her heart so much good to see that she and Grayson were falling in love. Rachel deserved a second chance at love.

She had a good drive back home to Columbus. As she walked in the front door, the phone was ringing. She dropped the picnic basket and grabbed the phone.

"Hello, this is the Hargrove residence."

"Patricia?" asked an unknown voice of a man, on the other end of the line.

"Yes, this is Pat. To whom am I speaking?" she asked.

"Patricia... this is Roman, " said the man.

"ROMAN??? ROMAN HUNTER???" she asked in disbelief.

"Yes."

"Where are you, Roman?" she asked.

"Here in Columbus," he replied.

"Why are you calling me?" she asked.

"Because I need to talk to you."

"We have nothing to talk about. You said it all long ago, when you left me standing at the altar over thirty five years ago. I thought you were probably dead by now. Do you honestly think I want to hear anything you have to say?" she asked.

"PLEASE... hear me out... PLEASE, don't hang up on me," he begged. " And NO... I am not dead."

"I won't hang up, but I have one question for you. What I really want to know is why didn't you show up for our wedding? Why did you humiliate me so badly? You broke my heart into a million pieces, and it took a long time for it to mend. Actually, I never got over it. I just tried to put it behind me."

"I am sooo sorry," he said. "PLEASE... hear my story!"

"I can't wait! I'm sure it will be a good one," she said sarcastically.

"First of all, I was on my way back to Columbus, the day before our wedding was to take place. I had a horrible car wreck in Billings. I was in the hospital for over 3 months, with most of the bones in my body broken. On top of that, I had amnesia. The bones finally healed, but the amnesia didn't go away at that time. I didn't know who I was, or where I had come from. It was a terrible feeling. I felt so helpless. Anyway, while I was in the hospital, a nice little nurse, named Julie became my very good friend. After I was released, we started dating. They had named me John Doe, in the hospital, so I kept the name John, and changed my last name to

Smith. John Doe was so generic. I asked Julie to marry me, and she said yes. A month later we were married. We were happy, for about two years, at which time, bits and pieces of my memory started to return. This was very disturbing! By the time I remembered you and our wedding that I had missed, I was in a deep depression. I had to tell Julie everything. She was very sympathetic, and tried to console me."

"Why didn't you call me then and let me know what had happened?" she asked.

"I thought about it, I truly did... but with me being married, I felt no good would come of it, so I wouldn't let myself call. I am so sorry! But I have to tell you Patricia, I never stopped loving you and I never forgot you, once my memory returned. Not one day went by, that I never thought of you, and the love we had shared," he stated.

"I'm glad you finally decided to tell me. I lived all those years wondering, and thinking you didn't love me enough to marry me, and skipped out on our wedding day," said Pat.

"I would never have done that! I wanted to marry you more than anything in the world!"

"I guess that makes me feel better, knowing the whole story. But why did you decide to tell me now?" she asked.

"Julie passed away six months ago."

"I'm so sorry," said Pat, and really meant it.

"My next question to you, Patricia... are you married?" Roman asked.

"No... I never married. I was hurt so badly, and decided I would never take the risk of being hurt again," she said with tears in her eyes.

"I am just so sorry, Patricia!"

They talked for an hour and it seemed like they had never been apart. Before they hung up, he told her he had another question for her.

"May I come over to see you after church tomorrow?" he asked.

She was speechless! This was all happening so suddenly. She hardly had time to take it all in. Before she could think, she blurted out, "Would you like to come over for lunch?"

"Yes, I would love that," he answered happily.

"Sounds good," said Pat. "I'll see you here at 1:00 p.m. for lunch.

"Thank you so much, Patricia."

"Please call me Pat. I haven't used the name Patricia for thirty five years."

"Okay, Pat. I'll see you tomorrow."

They hung up and she immediately called Rachel, who was stunned by the news. She had a million questions for Aunt Pat, but she waited and let her tell the whole story. There'd be time for questions later.

Pat was so excited, that she hardly slept that night. Finally morning came, and she was up early preparing food for lunch. She still couldn't believe it was true! She was afraid it was a dream, and she would wake up, to find it wasn't real. But, it was real!

She dressed in her prettiest blue suit, and left for church. She told no one of her invited guest. She was unusually cheerful, with a continuous smile on her face. Several people told her she sure looked happy. She told them it was a beautiful day. Oh, if only they knew, how beautiful it was about to be...

She kept checking her watch, hoping the preacher didn't see her. She had a hard time keeping her mind on his sermon, and felt bad about this. If only he knew what was on her mind, she was sure he would understand. Finally the service ended, and she hurried home. She was finishing the last minute touches, when she heard a car pull in her driveway. A tall, thin, gray haired man got out of his car, and walked toward her front door.

She couldn't wait... she met him on the porch.

"Pat," he said. "You look as beautiful as ever!"

"Thank you," she replied. "And you're as handsome as I remember. Where's my manners? Come on in."

"Thank you. It's so good to see you again," he stated, as he gave her a hug, and brief kiss on the cheek.

"You, too!" said Pat, blushing. "Lunch is ready, so have a seat."

He seated her, then himself. She said the blessing, thanking the Lord for allowing them to be together again. They talked as they ate, and afterward, he complimented her on the delicious meal.

She thanked him, and her face was glowing. She told him to think about what he had missed all these thirty five years. It was so good to have someone to cook for again. She'd missed that. Rachel had been gone for quite a number of years.

She put the food away, and he helped her with the dishes. They retired to the living room to chat. They had a lot of catching up to do. After several hours, he told her he had better go, and that he'd like to visit her again soon, if she was willing.

"Could you come for dinner next Saturday? I have some family I would like for you to meet. I know you remember Rachel, but she has a darling baby girl, named Jenny, who is my pride and joy."

"Yes, I can come, thank you," he said. I'll look forward to seeing Rachel and meeting her little daughter, Jenny."

As soon as he left, she called Rachel. After another lengthy conversation, she invited her, Grayson and Jenny to dinner next Saturday. Rachel accepted for all of them. She was very anxious to check out Roman... this man who had captured Aunt Pat's heart for the second time.

Rachel decided to call Grayson and make sure he would be available next Saturday. He said he would be there. With this off her mind, she decided to take Jenny out for a walk. She put her in the stroller, and headed for the barn. She checked on the horses. They loved for her to talk to them. Jenny was always excited to see the horses, too. Rachel knew Butch missed Mitch, but Rex and the cowhands, tried to fill in, when they had time. She and Jenny always went to the barn to check on them every evening. She wished she could ride Lilly more, but unless Aunt Pat was there, she couldn't leave Jenny.

Chapter 14

The next week passed quickly and it was Saturday again. She always looked forward to seeing Grayson, on Saturday or Sunday every weekend. He came over from Billings, early that afternoon. They enjoyed spending time together, just the three of them. Grayson was really getting attached to Jenny, and she to him. He would make a wonderful father for her, that is, if he asked her to marry him. So far, he hadn't asked. She was waiting...

They arrived at Aunt Pat's shortly before 5:00 p.m. Roman was already there. Grayson opened the door for her, and she got out. He then got Jenny out of her car seat, and carried her in. It all looked so natural. He was a natural born father. He was beaming as he carried her in the door. Rachel was beaming, too! She wondered how she could be so happy... again! In fact, she felt more in love with Grayson than she had been with Mitch. There was something different about him, from all other men, even Mitch. Maybe it had something to do with the way he loved and treated Jenny.

"Hello, Aunt Pat," said Rachel and Grayson in unison. They both hugged her.

"Hello, you two," she said.

"Come over here. I have someone I want you to meet," she said with a huge grin on her face.

"Roman, this is Rachel, her friend Grayson, and little Jenny," she said proudly.

"This is Roman Hunter."

"Hello Roman, nice to meet you," said Grayson, as the two men shook hands.

"Nice to see you again, Roman. What's it been... thirty five years?" asked Rachel.

"Nice to see you, too," he said, as he gave her a hug. "It's been way too long, that's for sure! Who is this beautiful little girl?" he asked, looking at Jenny.

"She's my pride and joy," answered Rachel.

"I think she is a family baby, as we all love her so much," said Grayson.

"You can say that again," said Aunt Pat.

Aunt Pat finished her dinner, along with Rachel's help, while the men talked and entertained Jenny.

They all sat down to eat, but not before Aunt Pat asked the blessing. She had so much to be thankful for. Actually, they all did!

Aunt Pat out did herself with the meal. She had so many dishes of food. It was hard to get around to tasting everything. She took pride in her cooking.

After they all finished and the kitchen was clean, they went to the living room to talk. After about 15 minutes of conversation, Roman announced that he had something special to say. The women held their breath... He pulled a box out of his pocket, got down on one knee, and proudly asked, "Pat, will you marry me?"

She was almost speechless... "For the second time, I say 'yes' to you, Roman Hunter." There was so much magic in the air at this moment. Rachel was so happy that the tears were rolling down her face. They were tears of joy... for her dear aunt, who had always sacrificed so much for her and Jenny. Now it was her turn to be happy and to be loved. To be loved by the only man, whom she had ever loved. This was more like a fairy tale ending.

Roman slipped the ring on her finger, and that's when she started crying. "I thought I was making you happy, Pat, and here you are crying."

It's tears of joy, my love," she told him.

"I want to get married as soon as possible. Rachel will you help Pat with the arrangements?"

"Of course, I will. Nothing would please me more."

"Grayson, will you be my best man?" asked Roman.

"I'd he honored to, sir," replied Grayson.

"You know I want you to be my maid of honor, Rachel," said Aunt Pat.

" I wouldn't have it any other way!" exclaimed Rachel.

"We want to go get married with just the five of us. I have no children, so you will be my family from now on. Pat, do you think we could get married in your church?"

"I'm sure Pastor Steve Weston would be happy to perform the ceremony for us," she said. "I will contact him right away. His wife Kathy can play the wedding music for us."

" Tell him you want the first available Saturday he has," said Roman.

"Are you in a hurry to marry me, Mr. Hunter?" she asked, smiling.

"You had better believe I am. We have wasted too many years already."

Pat and Rachel made the plans, and Pastor Steve was going to do the ceremony in two weeks. The girls had to get busy and find a dress. They decided to ride into Billings, where shopping was more plentiful. They found Aunt Pat a beige long dress, that flattered her slim figure. She looked lovely... Rachel found a pale pink dress, as this was the color scheme. She looked beautiful also.

Two weeks passed and the wedding day was here. Everyone was dressed in their new clothes. Jenny had a new pink dress, which looked very pretty with her dark hair. She was such a beautiful little girl. She had the opposite look of her mother, but was still very beautiful.

Everything went perfect at the wedding. The vows were said, and they were pronounced husband and wife. Then he was allowed to kiss his bride. They walked down the aisle, and out to the car. The reception was at Rachel's house on the ranch, with Rex and the cowboys joining them for the celebration. This story finally had a happy ending...

Chapter 15

Meanwhile, things were heating up with Rachel and Grayson. He had been thinking, and decided there was no use dragging things out. He knew this was the woman he was going to marry, so they might as well do it.

The next weekend, he came over and took Rachel on another picnic. He had to let Aunt Pat in on the secret, so she could keep Jenny. He asked Rachel if they could go horseback riding. This excited her, as she didn't get to ride as much as she liked. Aunt Pat and Roman came over to spend the day, and keep Jenny. Aunt Pat had a picnic basket in her hand when they arrived.

"Thanks for coming over to babysit, Aunt Pat and Roman. Also thanks for bringing the food," said Grayson.

"It's our pleasure," said Aunt Pat. "You two go… and have a good time. Take the picnic basket and enjoy."

"Oh we will!" said Rachel.

Grayson picked up the basket, and Rachel carried a blanket. They headed for the horse stable. Grayson saddled up Butch, while Rachel saddled Lilly. Grayson carried the picnic basket in front of him, while Rachel carried the blanket. Off they went, in a slow trot.

It was such a beautiful day to ride! They rode until they found the perfect picnic spot. It was under a big maple tree, with lots of shade, and near the babbling brook. There, they unloaded the picnic basket and blanket. They climbed back on their horses, and went for a long ride.

It had been quite awhile since Grayson had ridden a horse. Butch was well behaved, and was never a threat, to Grayson's relief. Grayson loved the wide open range... It was as close to God as you could get, being outdoors. It cleared your head and let you think straight. He was already thinking straight though, and knew what he was going to do today. Rachel had no idea.

They rode and rode... Rachel's beautiful, long blonde hair was blowing in the wind. She was a magnificent site to behold! She sat straight in the saddle, and you could tell she was not a beginner. She had been riding for a good number of years. She and Lilly had quite a connection. You could tell that by observing them.

Grayson was so happy he and Rachel had met. Today, he hoped she would agree to marry him. He knew she was the one for him. He had waited all these years for the right girl, and he had finally found her. Now... would she say 'yes' to his marriage proposal?

They rode back to the tree where they had left the picnic basket and blanket, and dismounted. They walked for a couple minutes, to stretch their legs. Then they spread the blanket on the ground, and started unpacking the basket. Aunt Pat had outdone herself again. She had made lots of delicious food for them. They were both starving. Grayson said the blessing before they ate. Rachel was so proud that he was a Christian, too! That would make life much easier for her, if they ever got married. The Bible speaks of this.

II Corinthians 6:14... "Be ye not unequally yoked together with unbelievers: for what fellowship hath righteousness with unrighteousness? and what communion hath light with darkness?"

After they finished eating, Grayson said, "I have a very special treat for you today." He reached in the basket, and pulled out a tiny black box. He opened it, got on one knee, and asked her, "Rachel Parker, will you marry me?"

The tears streamed down her face. She was so happy, she couldn't hold back the tears. "Yes, Grayson Sterling, I will marry you," she said breathlessly.

"Good... I was afraid you were going to turn me down," he said, teasing her.

"You wouldn't be that lucky," she teased. "You are everything I want in a husband. You will make me the happiest woman in the world, the day you marry me."

"That's why we need to do it as soon as possible. There's no use prolonging it."

"Sounds good to me," she added. "I will need a few months to get everything together. I don't want a large wedding."

"We'll do whatever you want," he replied.

"I think I would like to have an outdoor Western Wedding, here on the ranch, with family and close friends. I should be able to get things organized in four months. We'll hire a country band, who knows how to play square dance music, and make this an old fashioned wedding. Rex and the cowboys will like this, too!"

"I like the sound of that," he said. "I have always been a cowboy at heart anyway."

She looked at him... and thought, he does have that look, but much more handsome than the average cowboy. He was wearing a blue shirt that matched those piercing blue eyes, and he looked gorgeous! His black wavy hair and olive skin were the finishing touches. How was she ever so lucky to find this hunk of a man? Surely God was in the arrangements. Otherwise this good looking guy would already be married. She truly believed that God had prepared him for her.

"Aunt Pat, Jenny and I will go into Billings next Saturday, and check out the "Fancy Western Wear" store. They should have everything we need. I plan to buy a complete western outfit, even down to the hat and boots."

"Wow! You will make a beautiful cowgirl!" Grayson exclaimed. "As long as you marry me, I don't care what you wear."

"Thank you! I want this wedding to be perfect," she replied, smiling.

"I'm sure it will be, with you in charge," he said contentedly.

"I guess we had better get back to the house and share our good news," she said. So they packed up, and mounted their horses and headed back to the house. They were so extremely happy!

They walked in the door, with a big smile gracing their faces.

"She said YES!" he said excitedly, to Aunt Pat and Roman.

"Wonderful," they said in unison.

"When's the big day?" asked Aunt Pat.

"Soon... hopefully in about four months," replied Grayson.

"Aunt Pat, we need to go dress shopping in Billings next Saturday. We have decided to have a Western Wedding, here on the ranch, so I need to go to the 'Fancy Western Wear' store. Since I am asking you to be my matron of honor, you will need to look for a dress also."

"Oh yes, Rachel. I will be happy to stand up with you," replied Aunt Pat. " I will be excited to go shopping for a dress."

"Roman, will you be my Best Man?" asked Grayson.

"I'd be happy to," he replied.

So with that settled, they started talking wedding plans. They all loved the idea of a wedding on the ranch. This would be the first wedding to take place here.

Chapter 16

The following Saturday, Rachel, Aunt Pat and Jenny went to Billings. She found her size on the dress rack, and started browsing. Just as she was about to get to the next size up, there it was! She knew the minute she laid eyes on the dress, that it was the one for her. Now all she had to do, was go try it on, which she did. She came out of the fitting room, and people stopped and stared. She looked amazing! She had found the perfect dress. It fit her perfectly. It was white with rows of fringe, and white embroidery.

"So what do you think?" she asked.

"You look absolutely beautiful, Rachel! It's definitely the dress for you," replied Aunt Pat.

"Thanks," said Rachel. "Now I have to look for a hat and boots."

Two hours later, when they walked out of the store, they had everything they needed. Rachel had found her hat and boots. Aunt Pat had found a beautiful western dress also.

They headed back home to the ranch. It had been a fun,

yet eventful day. Jenny had been so good, and slept most of the time in the store.

Grayson and Roman were waiting for them back at the ranch. They were anxious to see if 'their girls' had found a dress, and were happy to hear that they had.

Things were falling into place. The band and photographer had been hired. A caterer was making up a menu for them, plus they were in charge of the cake. The flowers had been ordered and would be delivered the morning of the wedding.

Grayson and Roman went shopping together and both found nice western suits. The 'girls' were happy the men didn't procrastinate.

The wedding invitations were sent out a month in advance. Almost everyone had responded that they would be attending, including Grayson's parents, his older brother Tyler, and his younger sister Hannah, along with their families. Each one had two children. Rachel had never met any of them, so she was anxious to do just that. Grayson was taking her to Billings next weekend to meet all of them. He wanted her to meet them before the wedding. She was excited about going and hoped they would all like her.

Chapter 17

Next week came, and they drove into Billings. Grayson's father was in real estate and had done well for himself and his family. He owned his own company. None of the children worked for him though. Each one had their own career. His mother had always been a stay at home mom.

"I know my family will love you," said Grayson. He could tell Rachel was somewhat nervous at meeting them for the first time.

"I hope so!" she replied. "It is always difficult for me... meeting the family and wondering if they will like me or not."

"Just relax," he said. "You have nothing to worry about. I promise."

They pulled into the driveway at 1:00 p.m. Grayson's mom had invited them for dinner, but told them to come early so everyone would have time to talk before dinner. Tyler and his family were coming, as well as Hannah and her family. That was ten new people for her to meet... all at one time. No wonder she felt nervous.

Grayson got out of the car and came around to open her door. She got out and gave him a sweet smile. He took her hand, and said, "I love you! Everything will be fine! I won't leave your side."

That made her feel better. She took a deep breath as they walked up the front steps. Grayson's father came to the door. He was smiling, and that made Rachel feel more relaxed. "Hello," he said, as he opened the door.

"Dad, I'd like you to meet my fiancee, Rachel Parker," said Grayson.

"So pleased to meet you, Rachel," said Mr. Grayson. "Congratulations on your upcoming wedding. You're one lucky girl to catch my son," he teased.

"Nice to meet you, too, Mr. Grayson. Yes, I know I am very lucky to be marrying your son!" she exclaimed.

"Let's go find Mom," said Grayson.

Just then she walked into the living room. She took one look at Rachel, and gave her a big smile. "You must be Rachel... I've heard so many good things about you."

"Thank you, Mrs. Grayson. It's very nice to meet you, too," said Rachel, returning her smile.

"Oh, please... call me Marilyn," she suggested. "You can call my husband Bob, too. We don't like being formal. Everyone calls us by our first name, except our children," she laughed. I am so glad you could come for a visit before the wedding."

"Thanks, me too!" said Rachel. "I am anxious to meet the rest of your family."

"They should be here soon," said Marilyn.

A few minutes later, they all arrived close to the same

time. Tyler and Bethany got there first, along with their son Todd, and daughter Tiffany. A few minutes later, Hannah and her husband Jim arrived, along with their two sons, Joel and Aaron.

Introductions were made, and everyone was so nice and friendly. Soon Rachel felt at ease with all of them. She was going to love being in this family! She had no brothers or sisters, and she would be gaining one of each through marriage. She would also have parents again. It had been so long, that she could hardly remember what it was like when her mom and dad were alive. Of course, Aunt Pat had been a wonderful mom to her. She could never say otherwise.

Marilyn had a wonderful dinner and everyone enjoyed it immensely. Around 7:00 p.m., Grayson suggested it was time to leave. His parents asked them to spend the night, but they declined the offer. Rachel was uncomfortable about the situation, and besides, she was saving herself until marriage. True, she had been married before, but she was a virgin when she married Mitch. She wanted to be 'pure' for Grayson also. He understood!

They drove home in sheer happiness. Rachel was so happy that everyone seemed to like her, and Grayson was pleased as well. She already loved his family!

Chapter 18

The next few weeks passed and it was time for the rehearsal dinner, which was held at her house. They had a BBQ with all the trimmings. Everyone seemed to really enjoy themselves. Tomorrow was the big day!

Rachel woke up to beautiful rays of sunshine streaming in her window. Birds were singing in the trees, outside her window. What a glorious morning, she thought. This is my wedding day! It's finally here! I am the luckiest girl in the world. She jumped out of bed and looked at the clock. It was 8:00 o'clock. She didn't mean to sleep this late, but she didn't get in bed until after 12:00 last night. The rehearsal dinner had run way into the night. Part of the Grayson family was still here. Bob and Marilyn decided to stay with her, and the rest stayed at the Holiday Inn in Laurel. Grayson left about midnight and went home. He would pick up his suit and come back over tomorrow morning.

She could hear voices outside her window. As she looked out, she saw people scurrying about, getting things set up for the wedding, which would take place at 3:00 p.m. She knelt down by her bed, and prayed... thanking God for this day, and for sending Grayson to her. She knew it wasn't by accident. She asked God to be with them this day, and to protect everyone as they traveled to be with them on their special day. She asked a special blessing on Grayson, Jenny and herself, as they begin a new life together. She asked all this in the name of Jesus. She had such a peaceful feeling today. She knew God was in control of everything, including her life. She wanted to please Him in everything she would do today, and every day.

She saw that Grayson was already here, and was helping set up the chairs. His parents were helping him. What a lucky girl I am to be marrying into this wonderful family, she thought.

God surely has blessed me. They had really taken to Jenny last night when they met her. They both seemed so happy to be gaining another grandchild. Rachel was sure they would treat her equal to their other four grandchildren. That was also a blessing from God. Not everyone felt that way about step grandchildren. Rachel felt the Sterling's would never refer to Jenny as a stepchild, and she liked that.

She put on her robe and went downstairs to fix a pot of coffee. She saw that Marilyn had already done just that. She poured herself a cup, and sat down at the table, and reflected over the past several months. She wouldn't have dreamed she could have come so far, in such a short time. But, God was in control, not her... He said he would never put more on us than we could bear, but make a way of escape. Now, here she was... deeply in love, and about to marry the man of her dreams. Life couldn't get any better than this!

Her train of thought was broken, when Marilyn came in the kitchen door. "Good Morning, Rachel," she cheerfully said. "What a beautiful day for your wedding!"

"I know," said Rachel. "God has blessed us so much. I am the luckiest girl in the world to be marrying your son! You surely did a fine job raising him. He is a perfect gentleman!"

"Thank you, my dear." replied Marilyn. "Bob and I feel the same about you! We were beginning to wonder if Grayson would ever get married. He dated some, but never seemed to find a girl he wanted to marry, until you."

"I am so glad he never married! I feel that God was saving him for me."

"I am sure you are right. God knows the future and knows what each of us needs. It wasn't by chance that the two of you met, it was in His plan," said Marilyn.

"I totally agree with you, Marilyn!" said Rachel. "I never thought I could ever love again, after Mitch. God certainly has shown me I was wrong. I have learned that you should never say never. God has a way of changing our mind."

"That HE does," replied Marilyn. "I'd better get back outside and see if there is anything else I can do."

Rachel went back upstairs, and took a shower. She slipped into a pair of jeans and a T-shirt. She heard someone calling her name. It was Grayson. "Come on up," she yelled.

Grayson came bounding up the steps, taking two at a time. She could see he had a very excited look on his face. She figured it was because it was their wedding day, which was partly true, but he had some other great news, too.

"I have the most exciting news," he said so excitedly. "I just had a phone call from my boss. I got the promotion I had applied for! You know what that means, don't you? It means I won't be traveling anymore."

"That's great news!" exclaimed Rachel, with a beaming face.

"Now, I can travel to work each day, and be home at night, with you and Jenny."

"I am so very happy! Isn't God wonderful? He always does things in His own time. He knew what we were facing, and He fixed it for us. What a mighty God we serve!!!" exclaimed Rachel.

"That's for sure. He takes care of His own. I am so happy that we both are Christians," said Grayson.

"Me, too! It will make our marriage even stronger," she replied.

He gave her a kiss and went back downstairs. He was rejoicing over his good news. What a time to get this news, he thought. This makes our wedding day even more special. He went outside to see how things were coming along. It was looking good...

It was time for everyone to get dressed. Some used the downstairs bathroom, and some the upstairs bedrooms. There was plenty of room for everyone. Aunt Pat got dressed in Rachel's room, so she would be there to help her niece get dressed. Rachel was working on her makeup when Aunt Pat entered the room. With that finished, and her hair fixed, it was time to get into her fancy western dress. She slipped into the dress, and Aunt Pat zipped it for her. Next she put on her matching white boots, and cowboy hat. What a picture she made! Aunt Pat grabbed her camera, and started taking pictures. She took at least a dozen different poses.

"You are the most beautiful bride I have ever seen," she exclaimed. "You're even more beautiful now, than when you married Mitch.

"Thank you, Aunt Pat!" Rachel replied. "I am just as excited today, as I was when I married Mitch. What are the odds of finding two wonderful men?"

"When God is in control of your life... the odds are great."

"I want God to always be the center of my life," said Rachel.

It was 2:50 p.m., and they left Rachel's room, and went downstairs. She looked out the window and saw Rex, her foreman, who was giving her away. He looked handsome in his black western suit. He was so excited when Rachel asked him to give her away. He had never had the privilege of walking anyone down the aisle, so this was all new and exciting to him.

The band had already started playing music. Everyone seemed to be excited. Several of Rachel's friends were there, including Bill and Taylor, who was very pregnant. They looked so happy, and Taylor had that special mother-to-be glow on her face.

The rest of Grayson's family had arrived, and, were all looking very good. The seats were about full. Rachel saw Rex heading to the house. They would walk out the front door, and on to the white carpet runner, which would lead her to Grayson. Her heart was beating wildly...Just then the wedding music started and it was time to go. She took Rex's arm, and they started their walk into paradise.

"You look beautiful," said Rex. "Thank you for allowing me to give you away. I can do it, knowing you won't be leaving the ranch."

"I am honored to have you give me away, Rex. As far as leaving here, I have no plans to ever leave this place, as long as I'm alive. You will always have a job here, too!"

"Thanks Rachel. That sure is good to know. Don't know what I would do if I ever had to leave here," he said.

"Don't worry. You are here for good!"

Aunt Pat walked in just ahead of them...and took her place at the front. Roman was standing beside Grayson. They were all smiling...

She and Rex reached the front, and she stepped up beside Grayson, while Rex stepped back. After he had given her away, he was seated with the rest of the cowboys.

"You look absolutely beautiful," Grayson whispered to Rachel. She could tell he liked what he saw.

"You look very handsome," she whispered back to him.

The vows were said... spoken from the heart. Rachel and Grayson had written their own vows, which made it even more special. Grayson went first...

"Rachel, I have waited all my life for you! I knew from the first moment that I saw you at our friend's wedding... that you were the one for me. I knew my search for love was over. I had found the woman of my dreams... the one whom I want to spend the rest of my life with. I promise to be faithful, to love and cherish you and Jenny, and take care of you the rest of my life. I feel so honored that you are marrying me. I will love you forever!"

Rachel had been wiping the tears from her eyes as Grayson was saying his vows to her. He had put so much thought and his heart, into writing his vows. She prayed silently, "Dear God, thank you so much for sending this wonderful man to me. Let me always be worthy of him. In Jesus name I pray. Amen." Then it was time to say her vows to Grayson...

"Grayson, I told myself that I would never fall in love again. I honestly never thought I would... until you walked into my life. When we first met, and I looked into those piercing blue eyes, I was hooked. I knew that very day, that I had to get to know you better. Not one moment have I regretted my decision. When I see the love in your eyes, it melts my heart. You will not only make a wonderful husband for me, but also a great daddy for Jenny. We both love you so very much. I promise to be the best wife you could ever have. I will love and cherish you until the day I die."

The ceremony was over and the minister pronounced them husband and wife. Then came the famous words... YOU MAY KISS THE BRIDE... Grayson took advantage of this. He leaned her over and gave her a kiss unlike any she had ever experienced. She felt her face heating up. She heard people laughing...

"I now present to you, Mr. & Mrs. Grayson Sterling," said the minister.

They turned and began their walk back to the house, on the white carpet.

"We did it!" said Grayson. "Thank you for marrying me, Rachel!"

"I was most honored to do so, and I thank you for marrying me, too!" she exclaimed.

Jenny had seen her mommy walk by, and she squealed in delight. Roman went to get her as soon as the wedding was over. He had become very attached to her, in such a short time. She reached her arms to go to him, and gave him a big smile. She would be staying with him and Aunt Pat, while Rachel and Grayson went to Hawaii on a two week Honeymoon. They were really looking forward to keeping Jenny those two weeks. That would give them a chance to spoil her even more.

Wedding pictures were taken immediately after the ceremony. Rachel was hoping to get lots of good photos. With the land and the sky as the background, they had no option of being anything but good.

Everyone sauntered over to the reception area. There was so much good food...and each guest seemed to be enjoying themselves. Rachel was happy to see everyone eating and having fun. Soon it was time for the Bride and Groom to cut the Wedding Cake. This was always the fun part, watching them stuff each other's mouth full, which is just what they did.

The wedding was over, and most everyone was gone. The caterer was cleaning up and packing the uneaten food. Different family members were taking food, as Rachel and Grayson were leaving in the morning, and wouldn't be here to eat any of it.

Chapter 19

Everyone was gone... Aunt Pat and Roman had taken Jenny home with them. Now it was just Rachel and Grayson... alone at last. They went to bed around 10:00 p.m. and it was the most glorious night ever. They made passionate love for several hours. She was so glad they waited. It made it so much more special for both of them. They fell asleep in each others arms.

They were up very early the next morning. They had to drive into Billings, which was only 15 miles away, to catch their plane at 9:00 a.m. They had packed the night before, so they were on their way to the airport at 7:00 a.m. They boarded the plane on time, and were headed for Paradise!

They were staying at the Royal Lahaina Resort in Maui. It was set amidst 27 acres of tropical lawns and gardens, fronting the best and most exclusive stretch of Kaanapali Beach. This truly would be paradise!

They had several things planned to do. It would be a full two weeks. They got settled in their Hotel, and relaxed for about an hour, before walking on the beach. It was nearing sunset, which they didn't want to miss.

Tomorrow they were going to the Royal Lahaina Resort Luau. Rachel was really excited about this. But for tonight, they needed to get some sleep.

They woke to a beautiful sunrise. This had to be the most glorious place on earth! Neither of them had ever seen such a breathtaking sight. They got dressed and walked on the beach, looking for sea shells. They found some very pretty ones to take back home.

It was time to get ready for the Luau, so they got all dressed up in their Hawaiian clothes, and leis, and went outside to join lots of other people. Everyone was brightly dressed, which made a pretty picture. Of course, Rachel was snapping lots of pictures.

The menu included lots of delicious looking food. The main entree included, Kalua Pig, Kalua Turkey, Fresh Island Fish and Island Chicken.

Accompaniments were: Hawaiian Sweet Potatoes, Fried Rice, Corn, Seven Assorted Salads, Fresh Pineapple, Poi, Lomi Lomi Salmon, Taro and Guava Bread.

Desserts included, Coconut Cream Pie, Chocolate Cake, and Haupia (Hawaiian Pudding).

They ate things they had never tried before. It was all very delicious! They whole experience had been wonderful!

The next day they went for a drive. It was called 'Road to Hana', and was one of Maui's most beautiful drives through groves of bamboo and the ancient, organic, perfumed rainforests. There was a magnificent Pacific view along the way.

The next morning they saw the Haleakala Sunrise. Haleakala means, 'House of the Sun.' They understood why it was labeled as being so spectacular, after seeing it.

The 'Pools of Oheo', also known as THE SEVEN POOLS, were truly magnificent. Fed by pure mountain streams, these picturesque terraces of waterfalls and natural pools are the stuff of tropical dreams. The dense rainforest was the home to rare birds, who call out from the tree tops. The 'Pools of Oheo' is one of Maui's best-known attractions.

They got to see a Kapalua Beach Sunset, which was breathtaking. By day, this place was a lively crescent of sand, fringed with palm trees, in beautiful West Maui, and the perfect place to participate in Maui's favorite nightly ritual. Many other people traveled down the beach at dusk to see the sunset. One thing is for certain, no two are ever alike. The vivid nightly displays seem to last for hours, beginning with silver and golden hues, then painting the sky with lavenders, reds and purples... before cooling into a brilliant midnight blue.

At sunset, as torches were lit up and down the coast, the setting transforms from a tropical playground into a hushed, romantic enclave. Couples strolled the sands, hand in hand or snuggled up against the base of a palm tree to watch the stars come out. Rachel and Grayson did both. They were so happy and to be in the land of Paradise, made it even better. It didn't get any better than this!

Of course, they had to see a Volcano while in Maui. Standing at over 10,000 feet, it's not only Maui's most impressive natural landmark; it's the largest dormant volcano on Earth. Forming the entire base of East Maui, magnificent

Haleakala (House of Sun), and the surrounding Haleakala National Park, attract almost 1.5 million visitors a year. Rachel and Grayson were very happy to be included in this number.

The days were so fun filled, that the time was slipping away too quickly. They decided to do some 'Island Hopping'. The islands of Molokai and Lanai were wonderful one day trips.

Molokai is home to the world's tallest sea cliffs. It has miles and miles of untracked beaches. But what Molokai is most remembered for is the warmth and generosity of spirit displayed by its residents. They were told if they wanted to learn the difference between general friendliness and genuine Aloha, this was the place to go. They found it all to be true.

Just across the channel, beautiful Lanai boasts dramatic upland forests, a charming plantation-era town, and two of the most celebrated resorts in the Pacific. Lanai and Molokai were accessible by sea and air. Rachel and Grayson chose to 'island hop' via the scenic and relaxing ferry trips available from Lahaina.

They had heard about the Maui Onion Festival and decided this was something they had to do. The world famous Kula Onion exists in a taste category all its own. Also known as the Maui Sweet Onion - these bulbs were just that - sweet, crunchy, and delicious. The Maui Onion Festival was just the place to sample the many wonderful recipes this little vegetable had inspired. Attractions included chef demonstrations, live entertainment, games and prizes, and a produce market bursting with locally grown fruits and vegetables. They also had an onion eating contest. Grayson and Rachel decided they didn't want to participate in that. What a fun day they had...It didn't get any better than that!

In between all the different trips they took, they spent time on the beautiful white sandy beaches. They soaked up the sun, and Grayson's olive skin tanned so beautifully, and became even darker. With his black wavy hair and those sexy blues eyes, Rachel couldn't take her eyes off him. Not to mention how masculine and trim he looked in his swimming trunks. Lots of other women stared at him, too... but Rachel didn't mind, because she was the one going home with him. She was very proud to have such a good looking husband.

On the other hand, Rachel didn't realize how stunningly beautiful she was. Grayson knew though... and he watched how other men watched her also. She stood out from all the rest. No wonder the men liked to look at her; he didn't see another woman, that could even come close to her beauty. She had that long golden hair and green eyes unlike any he had ever seen before. They made your heart melt, when you looked into them. She had such an innocent look about her. Her skin was as smooth as porcelain, but she was getting brown from the sun. She wore a one piece swim suit, which accented her perfect figure. She would have looked stunning in a bikini, but she was far too modest for that. She didn't believe in showing that much of her body in public. That came from her upbringing.

They spent time on Makena Beach, which was one of Maui's premier beaches. Makena (also known as Big Beach) was a wonderful place to soak up the sun or catch a sensational Maui sunset.

All too soon, their two weeks had come to an end, and it was time to go home. What a memorable Honeymoon this had been. It was one they both would long remember.

"It's been a wonderful Honeymoon," Grayson told her. " I am so glad you married me, because I love you with all my heart!"

"I love you, too!" she told him. "This will be a memory that will remain in my mind as long as I live."

"Me, too!" he said. "This was more like something you read in a romance book, but it is real, and it happened to us."

"I know... and I am so thankful it did! I am so glad we found each other."

They had plenty of souvenirs to take home for themselves, as well as a Polynesian Doll, a Hawaiian outfit, among other things for Jenny, and gifts for Aunt Pat and Roman, too.

The next morning, they were up early, and caught a plane back to Montana. Rachel was anxious to see Jenny. It felt like she had been away from her forever. But she would wait, since they were late getting home. They both needed a good night's sleep, so tomorrow would be a good time for them to go pick up Jenny.

Chapter 20

Grayson had already told Rachel before the wedding that he wanted her to quit her job and stay home with Jenny. That made her very happy. She had always hated leaving her daughter, but had no choice. Things were really working out for her. This would be better for Aunt Pat, too. She could spend all her time with Roman, and build a life with him. They were both in their mid fifties, so they were getting a late start. The time they had left together would be precious to them. It's not the quantity of years you have together, but rather the quality of the years.

The next morning they were up early. Rex came to the house to welcome them home. He said everything ran smoothly while they were away. Rachel never worried about that, because she knew Rex would take care of everything. She was so blessed to have such a dependable foreman.

After breakfast, she and Grayson drove over to Columbus to pick up Jenny. It was a thirty minute drive. The sun was shining and all in all, it was a very pleasant day. They pulled in Aunt Pat's driveway, and parked the car. Before they could get out, the front door opened, and here came Aunt Pat, leading Jenny. Roman was right behind them. They all had big grins on their faces.

"Mommy!" yelled Jenny. "Mommy, I missed you!"

"I missed you too, Pumpkin!" said Rachel. "Come give mommy a big hug."

Jenny ran over to her, and gave her the biggest hug ever. She also kissed her on the cheek, and Rachel returned her kiss. It was so good to see her little daughter again.

"Do you have a hug for Grayson?" asked Rachel.

Jenny looked at him, and shyly walked over to where he stood. He bent down and picked her up, at which time she gave him a hug. He kissed her cheek and said, "Jenny, I love you!"

She smiled and wanted down. It would take her awhile to get used to him being around. He would work easy with her, and in time, she would accept him, and he would be the daddy she never had. He was actually looking forward to having a daughter. He loved Rachel so much, that accepting her daughter would be easy for him.

Jenny was about to turn three years old. She was getting to be a big girl now. Since Rachel was not working, that gave her more time to plan a party for Jenny. She still kept in touch with all her friends from Big Sky Real Estate Company, so she would have plenty of children to invite. Of course they were a few years older than Jenny, but they still loved to come to her parties. Rachel always had plenty of fun games, and good food to eat. Each child had a goody bag to take home with them. This had worked so well, Rachel knew there was no use changing the tradition.

Jenny's birthday came, and the party was a big success. The children had such a wonderful time. That pleased Rachel to see the children having fun. This was the first time Grayson had attended a party for Jenny. He had as much fun as the children.

Of course, Aunt Pat and Roman came, too. Since they worshiped the ground Jenny walked on, they wouldn't have missed her party for anything.

Chapter 21

It had been two months since Rachel and Grayson came back from their Honeymoon in Hawaii. She woke up one morning feeling nauseated. Oh no, she thought. I am coming down with a virus. She lay in bed for another few minutes, then got up. As soon as her feet hit the floor, she ran to the bathroom. She was so sick... I'm sure this will be over in twenty four hours, she thought. I hope Jenny and Grayson won't catch it from me.

For the next week, Rachel was sick every morning. Then it hit her... I'm pregnant again! She was overjoyed at the thought. They hadn't been trying, but never prevented it either. At her age, she needed to go ahead and have a baby, if they intended to have one. She would have been content to raise Jenny as an only child, but Grayson thought she needed a little brother or sister. Now that reality had set in, she was very excited. She would definitely tell Grayson her suspicions when he came home tonight. She would not put it off, like she did last time.

She called her doctor and made an appointment. He

would confirm what she already knew. Just a few more days...

Grayson came home from work to find a very excited Rachel. "You look like you have some good news," he said to her.

"Yes, I do," she replied.

"Well, I'm ready... what is it?" he asked.

"I think I'm pregnant!" she stated, excitedly.

"That is the most wonderful news I could hear!" he responded in an excited state. He grabbed her and gave her a big hug and kiss. He was so extremely happy!

"I knew you would be happy," she exclaimed.

"Am I ever!" he said excitedly. "When are you going to the doctor?" he asked.

"I have an appointment in three days."

"Have you told Jenny?" he asked

"Not yet. I want to wait and make sure it's true."

Finally three days passed and she went for her doctor visit. He confirmed her suspicions. She was definitely pregnant... a little over two months. Well, she thought... I must have gotten pregnant on our Honeymoon. That would be an exciting thing to tell the child when it was big enough to understand... How exciting to know you were conceived in Hawaii.

Rachel had a good pregnancy. She had no problems at all. Of course Aunt Pat and Roman were beside themselves with joy, when they found out. Rachel was so blessed to have them. She knew she could always count on them when she needed their help.

Month after month went by, and Rachel grew bigger

with child. She had found out she was having a baby boy. She was very happy about this. Grayson was overjoyed! So were his parents, Bob and Marilyn. They would have another grandson to carry on the Sterling name. It seemed that everyone was happy and were just waiting.

Finally the day came... The pains started during the night. She woke Grayson and told him it was time to go to the hospital. Aunt Pat and Roman had been staying with them for the past week, in the event Rachel went into labor early.

Rachel knocked on their door lightly. Aunt Pat was on her feet instantly. She opened the door, and asked, "Is it time?"

"Yes," replied Rachel. "We'll be leaving in a few minutes."

"Now don't you worry about a thing, Rachel. Roman and I will take care of everything. You just go have us a beautiful, healthy baby boy."

"I'll do my best," replied Rachel, as she turned and walked back to her bedroom. Grayson was dressed and had her overnight case in his hand. He was ready to go.

They arrived at the hospital about twenty minutes later. A male nurse met them with a wheelchair. Rachel sat down and started her journey...Grayson followed closely behind, carrying her overnight case.

She was in labor about 6 hours. Grayson never left her side. He wanted to be with her all the way. He had gone to every Lamaze class with her. She was so grateful for that. Mitch never had the pleasure of attending classes with her before she had Jenny. He died too soon! Thinking back, she wasn't sure if he could have been with her anyway. Being a doctor comes first. She needed to stop thinking back, and concentrate on the present. She was about to give birth to Grayson's son.

At exactly 8:00 a.m., Robert Grayson Sterling, made his entrance into the world. He was a big 7 lb. 15 oz baby. He had a head of thick black hair, just like his daddy, Rachel observed, as they laid him on her stomach. She fell in love with him the instant she saw him. In many ways, he reminded her of Jenny, especially the thick black hair.

Grayson was beside himself! She had never seen him so excited. He was walking on air... He had gotten the son he longed for. She closed her eyes, and thanked God for blessing them with this beautiful, healthy baby boy. She also asked God to bless the four of them with a happy, healthy home. She knew they always had to put God first in their lives.

A couple days later, Rachel and Robby got to come home. Little Jenny, was so very excited to see "her" baby. The first thing she wanted to do was hold him. Rachel sat down on the sofa beside her, and let her hold her new baby brother. The smile on her face was priceless, which Grayson was able to capture on the camera. That was one of those 'Kodak Moments.'

Chapter 22

Meanwhile, things were going well at the ranch. Everyone seemed to be very happy. Rachel had a wonderful husband, and two beautiful children. It couldn't get any better than this.

Rex, Rachel's foreman, hired a new boy to help on the ranch. He really wasn't looking for help, but this young boy of eighteen, showed up one day, looking for a job. Rex normally didn't hire anyone that young, but the boy seemed desperate for a job. He was a tall, slim, good looking young man, with black hair and brown eyes. His name was Jordan Hoffsteader. Rex had never seen him before, but there seemed to be something familiar about him. It seemed to Rex, that the boy should be in school, instead of working on a ranch. Against his better judgment, he hired Jordan.

Jordan settled in really well. He was a fast learner and got along well with the other cowboys. He seemed right at home here on the ranch. One day, Rex took him aside and told him they needed to talk.

"I haven't pried into your personal life, but I need to

know if you finished high school, or did you quit to go to work?" Rex asked him.

"I just graduated in June," Jordan replied. "I don't have money to go to college, so I had to find a job."

"Where did you come from?" asked Rex.

"Up north," he replied.

"You're a long way from home, aren't you?" asked Rex.

"Yes, but I always wanted to come west, and see a real ranch. "

"Why did you pick our ranch?" asked Rex.

"It looked like a good place to work, so I just stopped in to ask for a job."

Rex could see he was getting nowhere with him, so he told him he was doing a good job, and he was happy to have him join their crew.

This pleased Jordan, who instantly said, "Thank you, very much, Sir."

"You don't have to call me 'Sir'... my name is Rex. That is what everyone calls me."

"Okay, Rex," said Jordan. "You're a good boss. I am enjoying living here and working for you."

"Thanks, kid," replied Rex. "Now, let's get back to work."

Later that evening when work was finished, Jordan called his mother, Christina Hoffsteader. He tried to call her as often as he could. Since he was an only child, and she didn't have a husband, she was alone now.

"Hi Mom," he said as she answered the phone.

"Oh, hi Jordan... How are things going for you at the ranch? I sure do miss you!"

"I know, and I miss you, too. You know I had to do this, Mom!" he exclaimed.

"I know son... you're eighteen now, and I can't hold on to you forever," she said.

"Things are going well here. The ranch is beautiful, and Rex, the foreman is a good boss. The other cowboys are nice to me, and I seem to fit in very well."

"That's great," she said. "I'm so happy to hear that."

"Rachel and her husband Grayson treat me well also. They have two cute little children. Jenny is by Rachel's first marriage, and Robby is Grayson's son. They seem like a very happy family."

"I sure am glad to hear that you are being treated well," said Christina. "That was my biggest concern. I just need to know you are receiving good treatment."

"You don't have to worry, Mom. I will be fine. I think I have found a home," he replied.

"I hope you'll be happy."

"We'll talk later, Mom. I love you!" he said.

"I love you, too!" replied his mom.

"Bye for now, Mom."

"Goodbye son."

He put his phone away and went to the bunk house to join the rest of the cowboys. Most of them were talking and one cowboy was strumming his guitar.

Chapter 23

A year went by, and Jordan was still there. Rachel couldn't understand why a young good looking young man would want to spend his life being a cowboy. Surely there was much more out there for him. She decided to have a talk with him.

She called him to the house, and asked him to have a seat. She fixed a cup of coffee for both of them. He seemed a little nervous being in the house with her. Was she going to fire him? he wondered... He didn't want to leave the ranch. It seemed like home to him, and just the very place he was destined to be.

"I guess you are wondering why I asked you up to the house," she stated.

"I must admit, I am a bit curious," he replied.

"I don't know anything about you, but I have to ask you... what do you want out of life?"

"I'm afraid I don't understand," he replied.

"You seem like college material to me. I have to wonder why you want to keep working on a ranch."

"First of all, I don't have money for college, and I happen to like working here on your ranch," he said.

"What about your parents... can they not afford college for you?" asked Rachel.

"No, I only have a mom... I never knew my dad. They weren't married, and he never knew about me. Mom moved after she found out she was pregnant. She had to drop out of college and get a job. She never let him know about the pregnancy, or where she had moved. She wanted a clean break."

"My, this is sad... that he never knew about you. Do you think this is what he would have wanted?" she asked.

"I honestly don't know. My mom never told me anything about him until I was grown. She said he was a professional, and she didn't want to hold him back. They had met in college. That's why she dropped out of school and moved away."

"That surely was very unselfish of your mom," said Rachel.

"I know... I have a wonderful mom, who has always been there for me. I think she tried to be both mom and dad to me. She never dated anyone...her life was built around me."

"That's great, but she has made a tremendous sacrifice for you. I hope you never let her down," said Rachel.

"I don't plan to. I am saving every penny I can to go to college. That is what she really wanted for me. I came here to work and save."

"But why here?" asked Rachel.

"I wanted to come west and the Big Sky Country seemed like the perfect place to come."

"I'm glad you picked us," said Rachel.

"Me, too!" said Jordan.

"You're free to go now. I'm sure Rex has something for you to do."

"Thanks, Mrs. Sterling," he said.

"Just call me Rachel. The others all do," said Rachel.

"Okay... Thanks, Rachel."

"You're welcome, Jordan. Anytime you want to talk, I am here for you."

"Thanks, Rachel," he said.

Jordan got up and walked out the door. This had been a pleasant conversation. He wasn't nervous anymore. Rachel was a very nice Lady. He liked her. I am going to enjoy my stay here, he thought. He wasn't sure how long he would be here, but it surely was a pleasant place to work. He missed his mom, but he was 19 years old now, and had to make his own life. He wished she could come for a visit. He would love for her to see the ranch. Montana was so different from the northeast, where he came from.

Chapter 24

One day he decided to ask Rachel if his mom could come for a short visit. He went to the main house, and rang the door bell. Rachel came to the door, carrying baby Robby.

"May I have a minute with you, Rachel?" he asked.

"Of course, Jordan. Come in," she replied.

"I have been here over a year, and I know my mom misses me as much as I miss her. I was wondering if she could come for a visit? The only thing is... she can't stay with me in the bunk house, and I'm not sure she could afford a motel for a week."

"That's not a problem, Jordan. She can stay here with us. We would love to have her."

"Really?" asked Jordan, excitedly.

"Yes, really," said Rachel. "She would be most welcome."

"I can't wait to call and tell her!" he exclaimed. "Thank you so very much!"

That night he called Christina. She was so excited, and hardly knew what to say. She had been saving some money, and was sure she had enough to buy a round trip plane ticket.

Two weeks later, she was boarding a plane, heading for Montana. She had never been west, so this was very exciting for her. She had heard so much about Rachel and Grayson, from Jordan, that she felt like she already knew them. Jordan also talked about beautiful little dark haired Jenny, and baby Robby.

Robby looked more and more like his daddy, the older he got, and that made Grayson very proud. They had the same olive skin, black hair and piercing blue eyes. Grayson could never deny this baby... not that he would want to. Robby was a carbon copy of Grayson. Rachel was glad. She could see how happy it made Grayson, and she wanted him to be happy.

Jordan met his mom at the airport in Billings around 3:00 p.m. After some hugs and kisses, they headed for the ranch. Christina was a little nervous. Jordan tried to reassure her that all would be okay. Just as he said, all was great.

Rachel was at the front door to welcome Christina. She noticed the woman had dingy blonde hair, which was in need of color, and she looked very tired. She had to be at least five years older than Rachel. Or maybe she just looked older than she was. Rachel assumed life had not been easy for Christina. Rachel gave her a hug as she walked in the door.

"Hello Christina, and welcome to our home. I'm Rachel Sterling. We are very happy to have you visit us. I know it means so much to your son."

"Thank you, Rachel. It is so nice of you and your

husband to open up your home to a complete stranger," said Christina.

"Don't think of yourself as a stranger," said Rachel. "We're all one big happy family, here on the ranch."

"You'll never know how much this means to me. My son is all I have, and I have missed him so much. I prayed and asked God to make a way, for me to see him. The next day, Jordan called, and I knew God had heard my prayer," said Christina, with tears in her eyes.

"God does answer prayers! He has answered so many for me. There have been times in my life that I hardly knew which way to turn. When I called on the Lord, He was always there, waiting to work a miracle in my life. Believe me, when I tell you... He has done things for me, that I never thought would happen. I give Him all the honor and praise!"

"We can never praise Him enough! I know He works through other people, to help those who are in need."

"That is so true," said Rachel. "Well, you must want to freshen up, so I'll show you to your room. Follow me..." Rachel turned and started up the stairs with Christina following. "Supper will be ready at 5:00 p.m."

Rachel went back downstairs to the kitchen, and finished cooking supper. At exactly 5:00 p.m., Christina came down the steps. Rachel could tell she had been asleep.

"I'm sorry, Rachel! I meant to come down earlier and see if I could help you. I laid down for a few minutes, and didn't realize I had fallen asleep, until I looked at the clock a little before 5:00 p.m."

" Oh no, you did the right thing. I could tell you were tired, so don't feel one bit guilty." Jordan will be taking his meals with us while you are here. He always eats with Rex and the other cowboys in the bunk house. I want him to get to spend as much time with you as possible this coming week."

"I really appreciate that, Rachel," said Christina.

About that time Grayson walked in the front door. He was just getting home from work. He came straight to Rachel and gave her a kiss. Then he turned and introduced himself.

"Hi... I'm Grayson Sterling, Rachel's husband. Welcome to our home," he said.

"Hello, I'm Christina Hoffsteader, Jordan's mom," she replied. "Thank you so much for allowing me to stay in your beautiful home."

"You're very welcome. We're glad to have you. I know Jordan is excited that you came for a visit."

"Yes, he is, but probably not as excited as I am," she replied.

"Just make yourself at home."

"Thank you very much," said Christina.

They all gathered around the table. Grayson said the blessing before they ate. He thanked God for all His blessings, the food, and for the fellowship of Christina and Jordan.

Everyone seemed to enjoy Rachel's meal. She had the table filled with wonderful food. Aunt Pat had taught her well.

The week went by too quickly. Christina had such a wonderful time. During the day she and Rachel would do things together. They went shopping a couple times in Laurel. Then Rachel decided it would be nice to take her into Billings. Christina would be leaving tomorrow, and she wanted her last day to be special.

Rachel called Aunt Pat and asked if she would like to join them. Of course, they had to take the children, and she knew Aunt Pat would be lots of help with them.

The three of them, plus the two children left the ranch about 11:00 a.m. Billings was only a short drive, so they got there in plenty of time for lunch. They decided to go ahead and eat first. That way the children wouldn't get hungry.

Since McDonald's was the only place Jenny liked to go, they decided to please her. After they ate, she could play, while they talked awhile. Baby Robby would probably go to sleep in his stroller. The children were settled, and the three ladies began to talk. Not long into the conversation, Christina spoke up...

"Rachel, there is something I need to tell you. I know I should have told you when I first got here, but I kept waiting for the right time. Now my time has about run out, and I must tell you now."

"What is it, Christina? You have such a worried look on your face? Surely it can't be that bad!" said Rachel.

"I hardly know where to begin," said Christina.

"You know you can tell me anything, Christina," said Rachel.

"Okay, here it goes... You know I told you I dropped out of college, and moved away because I was pregnant. The truth is... I am from Boston, MA. I was going to Harvard when I got pregnant. My boyfriend was planning to become a doctor. I knew if we got married, it would be a struggle for him. So I put his needs before my own, and left him. He never knew I was pregnant."

"Wow," said Rachel. "What a sacrifice you made for him."

"I did what I felt like was the best at the time."

"Does Jordan know who his father is?" asked Rachel.

"Yes, I told him the day he turned sixteen. I thought when he got older that he might want to find his father. But I waited too late. One of my friends from college kept in touch. She was the only one who knew the real reason for my leaving Boston. A few years later, she called me and said that Jordan's dad was dead."

"Oh, that is awful!" said Rachel.

"I grieved for him, even though it had been over a long time ago. I guess what hurt me the most, was the fact that Jordan would never have the chance to meet his dad. What I have to tell you now, Rachel, is that Mitch Parker was Jordan's dad..."

"Whaaat?" asked Rachel, in disbelief.

"Yes, it is true... Mitch was the father of my son."

"This is hard to believe," exclaimed Rachel.

"I knew it would be very difficult for you Rachel, and I am so sorry to hurt you. I felt like it was time to tell the truth. This is the reason Jordan showed up at your ranch. He wanted to see where his dad had lived. He wanted to meet you and his little sister. What he didn't plan on, was falling in love with the ranch and the life here. He loves you, Rachel. He said you had been very good to him."

"Jordan is a special boy!" said Rachel. "I took to him from the first moment I met him. Now I am thinking maybe it was because he was a part of Mitch, even though I didn't know it at the time. Wow...this is a lot to digest."

"I know," said Christina. "You have been so good to me, and I felt like you deserved to know the truth."

"So this makes another child that Mitch never knew about. That really makes me sad. I had planned to tell him about my pregnancy the night he got killed. I have regretted it so many times, that I never told him when I first found out. If only I could do it all over..."

"The past is gone, and neither of us can do anything about it," said Christina. "What I want to know now is... will this affect your relationship with Jordan? Will you want him to leave the ranch?"

"Goodness, no...," said Rachel. "If anything, it will make me feel closer to Jordan, by him being a part of Mitch."

"I'm glad to hear that. I have been worried about that," said Christina.

"You can quit worrying now!" said Rachel. "If Jordan wants to stay on here, he will become a part of our family."

"Oh, that is wonderful!" exclaimed Christina. "I am sure that is what he will want. He already thinks so highly of Grayson, who has been a father figure to him."

"Then I don't see a problem," said Rachel. "I want you to know, you are welcome to come visit us anytime you choose."

"Thank you so much, Rachel. You are a wonderful woman!" said Christina.

Rachel turned to Aunt Pat, who had kept silent the whole time. "It looks like we have another son, doesn't it?

"Yes, this is an amazing story. We've had many amazing things happen to us in the past few years," said Aunt Pat.

"I know... that proves you never know what the future holds... you only know WHO holds the future," said Rachel.

They left the table, each one in a different state of mind, from when they sat down. Christina felt excitement and relief, just knowing that Rachel had accepted Jordan. Rachel felt happiness knowing Jordan was Mitch's son, and also sadness, that Mitch had never known him. She truly hoped that he would continue to stay here on the ranch. She would tell Grayson the news tonight. She already had an idea running through her head...

The women had a good time shopping and each one found several things. After three hours, they decided that was enough, and headed back to the ranch.

Rachel stopped at KFC on the way home and bought supper. That would be easier, since she was already tired. After they had eaten, Christina retired to her room to pack for her departure tomorrow. It had been a lovely week...

Chapter 25

Rachel got the children bathed and in bed, then she and Grayson retired to the family room. Rachel knew she wanted to tell him the news right away.

"Grayson, we had an eventful day in Billings today. I learned a secret that was really shocking to me."

"What kind of secret?" he asked.

"Christina told me the father of her son, Jordan," she said.

"Why would she do that?" asked Grayson.

"Because it has something to do with us," she replied.

"What do you mean?" he asked.

"Jordan is Mitch's son," said Rachel.

"You're kidding, right?"

"No, I'm afraid not. Christina told me the whole story. Mitch never knew she was pregnant. He never knew he had a son."

"Wow... that's some heavy stuff."

"I know... what hurts me is that Mitch never knew about his son, or his daughter."

"That is tough!" exclaimed Grayson.

"So what do you think Jordan will do? Will he stay on here, or what?"

"I don't know... but I hope so. I have something I would like to discuss with you."

"I'm listening," said Grayson.

"Do you remember me telling you that Jordan is trying to save up enough money to go to college?"

"Yes, I think you did mention it."

"Well, I was thinking... I would like for us to pay for his college," said Rachel.

"Do you think he would accept our help?" asked Grayson.

"I don't know. I would have to talk to him. Maybe we can ask him up to the house tomorrow night and both of us have a talk with him."

"That sounds good," said Grayson.

"I will invite him to supper," she said.

"That sounds like a good idea."

The next day, Jordan drove his mom to the airport. They said their sad goodbyes and she boarded the plane. She knew she could come back anytime she could afford it, so that made leaving easier. She was so thankful that Rachel had accepted her and Jordan. Thank you, God, she prayed silently.

When Jordan returned home, Rachel walked down to the bunk house, and invited him to supper. She told him that she and Grayson had something they wanted to discuss with him. He went with her immediately, wondering what on earth they had on their minds. Grayson was in the den waiting for them. They both were seated, and Rachel started the conversation.

"Jordan, I guess you are wondering what we want to talk to you about," said Rachel.

"Yes, I am wondering," replied Jordan, with an uneasy look on his face.

Rachel could see the apprehension, so she decided to get right to the point. "We know that your father is Mitch Parker."

With a surprised look on his face, he replied, "You do?"

"Yes, your mother told me, the last day she was here."

"She never told me that she told you," said Jordan, wondering... "She never even told me until I was sixteen. I had asked her about my dad for many years, and she always changed the subject. The only thing she would say was she would tell me when I was grown."

"Why didn't you tell us when you first came to work here?" she asked.

"I was afraid you wouldn't hire me," he said nervously. "I just had to come see where my dad had lived. When I got here, I fell in love with the ranch, and your family, too!

Grayson had been listening, and decided to add his thoughts. "Jordan, you are very welcome to stay here. In fact, we would like for you to move into the house with us, and be part of our family."

His eyes widened and his mouth gapped open... "You do?" He couldn't believe what he was hearing. He had always wanted to have a family. He had missed not having a dad. Now he would have another mom, a dad, a sister and a brother. How lucky can one boy get?

"We would also like to talk to you about college," said Grayson.

"I have been trying to save as much money as I can toward college," replied Jordan.

"Rachel and I want to pay for your college education," said Grayson.

Tears welled up in his eyes..."Wow! I can't believe that! You are just too kind," he exclaimed.

"It's true," said Grayson. "Rachel really has grown attached to you, and after she found out you are Mitch's son, she said she wanted to do this for you."

"This sounds too good to be true!" he exclaimed, wiping his eyes.

"What are you interested in doing, or have you decided yet?" asked Grayson.

"I have known since I was in high school. What I would really love to do, is get into a Pharmaceutical School. Is there one near here?" he asked.

"You could take a two year course at Montana State University, then transfer somewhere else, or you could go to the University of Montana, located in Missoula. It is about 350 miles west of here."

"What would you advise me to do?" asked Jordan.

"I think it would be better to get all your schooling at the same university," said Grayson. "But we will leave it up to you,"

"I think you are right, about getting my education at one school. I never dreamed it would happen this soon, if ever. Thank you so very much!"

"We want you to be happy," said Rachel. "We will go

along with whatever you decide. You can think about it, and when you decide, we will start making preparations."

It didn't take Jordan long to decide. He thought the University of Montana in Missoula was the place he wanted to go. Meanwhile, he was busy moving his few clothes and things into the main house. He was very excited about this. Never in his wildest dream, did he ever think he would be living here, and be part of their family. God was so good! He had been praying about this situation for a long time. God had answered his prayers!

Chapter 26

Rex and the other cowboys hated to see him leave "their" family at the bunkhouse, but they fully understood, and were happy for him. Rex would not hire a replacement for him, as they really didn't need any more help. Actually, they never needed him, but he seemed so desperate, that Rex couldn't turn him away. He was glad he didn't... especially after finding out he was Mitch's son.

Meanwhile, Rachel was busy calling the university, and getting information for Jordan. He had to fill out lots of papers, before he would know if he got accepted. He prayed about this, too! He asked God to show him the right way to go. If this was right for him, he knew God would work it all out.

Two months after all the paperwork had been sent in, Rachel got a call from the university. Jordan had been accepted and would begin school in the fall. That was three months away, so that left time to get everything together and get him moved into the dorm.

Rachel took Jordan shopping for new clothes. He was so excited! She bought him several new outfits, shoes, underwear, and all the extras he would be needing. He was like a kid in a candy store... Rachel loved seeing the excitement on his face. That was worth every penny she spent on him. This brought back memories of when she was ten, and Aunt Pat had taken her to buy new things for her bedroom. She thought she knew exactly how Jordan felt.

The summer passed quickly. Grayson, Rachel, Jordan, Jenny and Robby, went on several day trips to various places. Every Sunday afternoon after church, they always had a picnic, if it wasn't raining. Most of the time they went to Rachel's favorite place, where Grayson had proposed to her. That would always be a special place to her.

About two weeks before Jordan was due to leave for college, a phone call came during the early morning hours. Rachel answered the phone in her usual pleasant voice. "Hello... Sterling Residence," she said.

"I am a friend of Christiana Hoffsteader's, and I have some bad news," said the voice on the other end of the line.

"What is wrong?" asked Rachel in a shaken voice.

"I am sorry to have to tell you, but Christina is dead."

"What?" asked Rachel in a shrill voice. "What happened?"

"She had a heart attack. She died before the ambulance could get to her home."

"Oh, I am so sorry! I dread to have to tell Jordan. Have any arrangements been made?"

"I don't think so. She had no burial plot and no money. I don't know what will happen," said the stranger.

"Can you give me the name and phone number of the funeral home that has her body?" asked Rachel.

"Just a minute and I will look in the phone book," said the stranger. "Hold on for a few minutes."

"I can wait," said Rachel.

Grayson was awake by now and asked Rachel what was wrong. After telling him everything the stranger had told her, he said. "Let's have her flown back here, and we'll have a local funeral home do the arrangements, then we'll bury her in our family cemetery, here on the ranch. We can bury her beside Mitch."

Rachel thought a minute, and replied."That is a good idea. I agree with you. This is where she belongs." The stranger came back to the phone.

She gave Rachel the name and phone number of the funeral home. Rachel thanked her and hung up the phone.

She wouldn't wake Jordan now, but would tell him as soon as he got up. She also had to call the funeral home in Boston, and make arrangements to have Christina's body flown to Billings. She would call Johnston Funeral Home in Laurel, and ask them to pick her up and make all the arrangements for her funeral. Rachel hadn't had time to think about the impact this was going to have on Jordan. It brought back memories to when she lost both her parents. It was a very difficult time in her life. She was so glad Jordan was here with them, so they could lend a shoulder for him to cry on. He was part of their family now, and he would never be alone again. She would see to that...

Jordan was up by 7:00 a.m. He came into the kitchen where Rachel and Grayson were having coffee. "Good morning," he said.

"Good morning," said Rachel and Grayson in unison.

"Would you like a cup of coffee?" asked Rachel.

"Yes, please," he answered.

Rachel got up and poured him a cup of coffee. "We have something we need to talk to you about," stated Rachel.

"Okay," said Jordan.

"We received a phone call early this morning from Boston."

"Was it my mom?" asked Jordan.

"No, it wasn't your mom, but was a friend of hers," said Rachel.

"Is something wrong?" asked Jordan, with a fearful look on his face.

"I'm afraid so," said Grayson. "Your mom had a heart attack last night and died before they could get her to the hospital. We are so sorry!"

"I can't believe it! My mom is gone?" he cried.

"It was a shock to us also. But we have something to tell you that hopefully will make you feel some better. We are having her body flown to Billings and our local funeral home will pick her up. The funeral will be here in Laurel, and she will be buried here on the ranch in the Parker Family Cemetery. She will be buried beside your father, Mitch. Your parents will be together."

"Thank you so much! I am so happy that you did this. It will make things a lot easier for all of us, not having to travel to Boston. I can't thank you enough! You people are just too good to me! At least I can visit her grave, and my dad's too," he said, wiping the tears from his eyes.

Rachel put her arms around him, and he laid his head on her shoulder. "We can never be too good to you," said Rachel.

"After all you are Mitch's son. Even before I knew the truth, I really liked you. Now that I know, I can see a lot of qualities in you that came from your dad. You will always be part of our family, Jordan... Don't you ever forget that!"

This pleased Jordan... He never dreamed this family that he had searched for, would be so kind to him. He was greatly blessed. He knew that God had sent him to them, to prepare him for the loss of his mom. Otherwise, he would have been alone. Now he had a wonderful family. He would miss his mom greatly, but it was much easier being here, than being alone. He had so many things to be grateful for.

The next few days were stressful, but with the Lord's help, they all made it through the funeral. Christina was laid to rest beside Mitch, the love of her life, from long ago. This never bothered Rachel at all. She would be buried on the other side of Mitch. In fact, she would be buried between her two wonderful husbands. That may sound weird, but that was the way she wanted it, and that's the way it would be.

It was getting close time for Jordan to go off to college. There was one more thing that Rachel wanted to discuss with him before he left. She had been thinking and praying about it, and knew in her heart it was the right thing to do. That is... if he agreed with her.

Chapter 27

After they finished supper, she told him they had another issue they wished to discuss with him. She got the kitchen cleaned, with Grayson's help, then they took the children upstairs to give them a bath, read a bedtime story and put them to bed. Grayson was so much help with the children, and he loved doing it. He was so proud to be a daddy! Rachel was so thankful that God had given her such a wonderful husband. He had made a wonderful daddy, too.

With Jenny and Robby in bed, Rachel and Grayson came back downstairs. Jordan was waiting for them in the den. "Jordan, Rachel and I have been talking and we want to get your opinion on this matter. Since Mitch is your dad, we think it would be good if you had his name. Keep in mind, that doesn't mean we have anything against your name now, but you are a Parker, and we thought it would be good if you would consider changing your last name. That way you could carry on the family lineage."

"Wow... that is a lot to think about!" he exclaimed.

"We know that, and we don't want an answer now. Take your time and think about it. When you are ready, you can let us know your decision," said Grayson.

"I will consider it," said Jordan.

Jordan didn't sleep much that night. He kept rolling the idea over and over in his mind. His mother was gone... and she would never know. He was rightfully a Parker, and why shouldn't he carry the name? Finally about daybreak, he went to sleep. He knew what his decision would be. He would tell Rachel and Grayson after he got up.

They were already up and about when he entered the kitchen around 9:00 a.m. Even Jenny and Robby had gotten up before him. "Good Morning, everyone," he said to all of them.

"Good Morning to you," said Rachel. "How did you sleep last night?"

"I didn't sleep much. I had too much on my mind to sleep. I didn't mean to sleep this late, but it was late when I finally went to sleep."

"We understand," said Grayson. "We know you had a lot on your mind."

"Yes, I did and I have come to a decision. I want to take my dad's name."

"That is great!" exclaimed Rachel joyfully. "I am so happy about your decision!"

"I think it will be for the best, too. Now Jenny won't be the only Parker in the house," he said laughing.

"That's right," said Rachel. "I know she will be happy about that when she gets old enough to understand."

"We'll get right on it. I will call my lawyer today and

set up an appointment for the three of us. I will tell him we need to do this before you leave for college."

"That sounds good to me," said Jordan.

When Grayson came home that afternoon, he had a look of delight on his face. Rachel wondered what was on his mind. It didn't take long for her to find out...

"I talked to my lawyer, and we have an appointment in two days."

"That's wonderful!" exclaimed Rachel. "I can't wait to tell Jordan."

Jordan had finished work for the day, and was taking a shower. When he came downstairs for supper, he could see excitement on Rachel and Grayson's faces.

"Jordan," said Grayson. "We have an appointment with my lawyer in two days. We will get this thing rolling. He understands our need to have this done as soon as possible."

"Wow... I'm excited!" exclaimed Jordan.

"My lawyer said he would have all the necessary paperwork ready for you to sign when we go this time. I told him you would be away at college and couldn't come back every time he needed a paper signed. He understood and told me not to worry... that he would take care of everything. You will soon have your rightful name, Jordan Parker!"

"I like the sound of that," he said grinning.

"You are already one of us, but that will make you feel it even more," said Grayson.

"I think you are right," he said, still grinning.

"We are so happy to have you as a part of our family, Jordan," said Rachel cheerfully.

"Thank you! I am happy to be part of your family," he stated.

Chapter 28

Grayson, Rachel and the children drove Jordan to Missoula to get started in college at the University of Montana. He was very excited. He was about to start his education, and fulfill his dream of doing pharmaceutical research. He couldn't believe all that happened to him in the past year. He now had a family, knew who his biological dad was, had taken his name, and was beginning the education he thought would be several years away, if ever. Life was good! He gave God all the praise for everything.

It was a long ride, so they got an early start. The children would probably sleep during the trip. It would take about seven or eight hours to get there. Rachel had made reservations for her, Grayson, Jenny and Robby to spend the night there. It was too much to drive back the same day.

They arrived at the college about around 4:00 p.m. They got Jordan settled in the dorm, and then they all went out to eat. Afterward they took him back to the college, said their sad goodbyes, then went to their hotel. They were all tired. They bathed the children, and put them to bed. That gave

Rachel and Grayson some alone time, to reflect over the past several days, and even the past year. They would never have dreamed that their lives would change so much. They were very happy and thankful for their three children.

The next morning Rachel woke up nauseated. It must have been something I ate for supper last night, she thought. The sick feeling wore off later in the day and she never thought any more about it. Until... the next morning, and she felt the same way. She dreaded the ride home. It would be unpleasant with her being sick. After she threw up a couple times she felt better. The ride home was pleasant... The children were good, and slept most of the way.

They stopped on the way home and ate, so Rachel wouldn't have to cook. Grayson knew she wasn't feeling well. Later when they arrived home, she got the children to bed early, so she and Grayson would have some time to relax.

"How are you feeling, now?" he asked.

"Better, I think, although I still have a little nausea," she replied.

"Hopefully you will feel better in the morning," he said.

"I sure hope so," she stated. "This reminds me of my pregnancy days."

"You don't think?" and she interrupted him.

"No, I don't think," she answered quickly.

The next morning as soon as her feet hit the floor, she went running toward the bathroom. She threw up again.

Grayson came in the door and asked, "Are you sure you are okay?"

"I don't know what is the matter with me," she stated, and then threw up again.

"I think you need to see your doctor. I will call work and tell them I can't come in today. The children and I will drive you into Laurel."

"Okay," she said and threw up for the third time. "I guess I do need to go."

Two hours later they were heading to the doctor's office. Rachel had called earlier and had been told to come on in.

They sat in the waiting room about half an hour, and the nurse came to get Rachel. After about forty five minutes, she came walking out the door, with tears in her eyes.

"What's wrong?" asked Grayson, with a deep look of concern on his face.

"You were right," she said, tearfully. "I'm pregnant! I'm thirty nine years old and going to have another baby."

"That's great news!" exclaimed Grayson, with a big grin on his face.

"I am just very surprised," said Rachel. "It will take some getting used to the idea of having another baby in the house. Robby is still a baby, too."

"We'll manage," said Grayson. "It had to be in God's will for us to have another baby. Otherwise, He wouldn't give it to us."

"I know..." said Rachel. "I know that God is in control and does what's best for us."

"I will just have to help you more around the house, and try to make things easier for you," said Grayson.

"You do so much already. I don't expect you to work all day, come home and do my work, too," she said.

"There's no reason I can't help. I'm the reason you're in this condition," he teased.

"It's both of us. I won't blame it all on you."

"We'll make it. As long as we have each other, and put God first in our lives, we will be fine," stated Grayson.

"I know... we must never forget who is in control. Anyway, after I get over this morning sickness, I can enjoy my pregnancy more. I will be excited to have another baby. I don't care if it's a boy or girl, as long as it's healthy."

"That's all that matters," said Grayson. "We will accept whichever God gives us."

"Since we already have two boys, it would be nice to have another little girl."

"That's exactly what I was thinking," said Grayson.

They all left the doctor's office and headed for home. On the way they stopped at McDonalds's and got the children their favorite food. They always had to have a Happy Meal. Rachel and Grayson settled for a Grilled Chicken Sandwich.

After they arrived home, Grayson helped Rachel bathe the children, and get them ready for bed. He read to Robby, while she read to Jenny. After tucking them snuggly into bed, they went back downstairs.

"I have to call Aunt Pat and let her know our news," said Rachel.

"Do you think she will be shocked?" asked Grayson.

"I really don't know," replied Rachel. "I think she will be happy to have another baby in the family."

Rachel dialed the number. Aunt Pat answered on the second ring.

"Hunter's residence," she said.

"Aunt Pat, it's Rachel."

"Oh hello Rachel. How is everyone?"

"We're fine... I do have some news to tell you though," said Rachel.

"I'm listening," said her aunt.

"Are you sitting down?" asked Rachel.

"No, do I really need to?"

"You might need to... I'm pregnant!" exclaimed Rachel.

"You're what?" asked Aunt Pat in a shrill voice.

"I'm pregnant."

"I heard you the first time. I just couldn't believe it."

"You had better get used to it, because it's true," said Rachel.

"When did you find out?" asked her aunt.

"Today," said Rachel.

"Well, I am very happy for you and Grayson. But I kind of worry about you being thirty nine and having another baby," said her aunt.

"I'll be fine. The doctor said everything looks good, and there is no reason I can't have a normal pregnancy."

"I sure am glad to hear that. We'll just all have to pray for you and the baby."

"I know, and we will. If God didn't want us to have this baby, He wouldn't be giving it to us."

"That is so true, Rachel."

Aunt Pat congratulated them, and told Rachel she was very excited for them.

Chapter 29

Things went well with Rachel's pregnancy. She actually felt really well, despite her age, and the fact that she had baby Robby to care for. Jenny was getting bigger, and could help out some, when she wasn't at school.

Jenny was six years old now, and was in first grade. She loved school and was really very smart. She was learning so much... One thing she really loved was art. She could draw amazingly well for a six year old. Grayson was quite an artist himself, so he encouraged Jenny a lot. He bought her some really neat art supplies. Through their love for art, they had bonded even more. Rachel was happy to see this. She was also happy that Grayson showed no partiality with the two children, even though he was not Jenny's biological dad. He was the only dad Jenny had ever known, and she loved him very much.

Grayson was excited about the new baby. He was going with Rachel to the doctor tomorrow for her sonogram. Neither of them had any preference of a boy or girl. Rachel would be forty years old by the time the baby was born, so they just prayed for a healthy baby, and that Rachel would have a safe, easy delivery.

The sonogram was scheduled for 11:00 a.m. Aunt Pat came over to keep Robby. Jenny was at school. It was five minutes past 11:00 when they were called into the room for the test.

Rachel lay on the table anxiously waiting, as Grayson stood by her side, holding her hand. Both were silently praying that everything would be normal.

"Mr. & Mrs. Sterling...it looks like you are going to have a baby girl," said the doctor. "Everything looks normal, and there's no reason you shouldn't have a normal delivery."

"Thank you, God, and thank you doctor!" exclaimed Rachel.

"That is wonderful news," said Grayson, happily.

"Rachel, I think one of you needs to consider surgery after this baby is born. Since you will be forty, it is in your best interest to not have any more babies," spoke the doctor, frankly.

"I will have it..." said Grayson. "It will be a lot easier for me than for Rachel."

"Sounds like a wise decision, Mr. Sterling," said the doctor.

They thanked the doctor and left. Rachel was so excited that she would be having another girl. Jenny would have a sister. Now their family would be complete, with two boys and two girls. God had blessed them so greatly!

Rachel couldn't wait to tell Aunt Pat the news. Somehow she knew her aunt would really be happy. It was a short ride back to the ranch. Aunt Pat met them at the door, with Robby in her arms. "Well..., what are we having?" she asked impatiently.

"We're having a girl!" exclaimed Rachel, excitedly.

"Ooooh... that is wonderful news. I am so happy for us. We need another girl, and Jenny needs a little sister."

"It looks like she will be getting one."

"Is everything okay with you and the baby?" asked Aunt Pat.

"The doctor said everything looks fine. He also advised one of us to have surgery, so I won't have any more babies. After all, I will be forty when this one is born."

"I agree with the doctor. You don't need to go through this anymore."

"I am going to have the surgery, in case you are wondering, Aunt Pat," said Grayson, laughing.

"I think that is admirable of you, Grayson. So many men would not be willing to do this."

"It is for the love of Rachel, that I am doing it. I don't want her to go through any more than she has to. She will deliver this baby, and hopefully her body can rest after that. Our family will be complete, and we will spend the rest of our lives raising these God given children, and hopefully one day, they will give us grandchildren to spoil and help raise."

"You are quite a man, Grayson Sterling!" exclaimed Aunt Pat. "I am so glad you and Rachel found each other. I know that was another part of God's plan."

"Me, too," said Grayson. "I was waiting for the right girl to come along, and I knew God would send her, when the time was right. Everything is done in His time."

"You are so right," said Aunt Pat. "Sometimes we get too anxious, and think about giving up, but we must wait on God. He has plans for all of us."

"I had given up on love," stated Rachel. "I just knew there would never be anyone else that I could love after Mitch. God sure changed my mind, didn't he? Now look at me... married again... to a wonderful husband, and soon to have his second baby. Who would have ever dreamed it would turn out this way? I know I certainly didn't."

"I'm glad God holds the future, and not us," said Grayson.

"Amen to that!" exclaimed Aunt Pat. "Just look how God sent Roman back to me after thirty five years! I would never have dreamed in a million years that would happen."

"We're two lucky and blessed women, aren't we?" laughed Rachel.

"We sure are, and we must never forget it," said Aunt Pat.

"I don't think we ever will," stated Rachel.

"Make sure you don't," teased Grayson.

Chapter 30

The next few months passed and Rachel was feeling well, except for getting heavier. She was planning Robby's birthday party, which would be in another week. She asked her aunt for help, which she gladly gave. Aunt Pat always got a thrill from helping with the children's parties.

Robby would be two years old on November 4th. He was getting to be such a big boy, and looked more like his daddy every day. Grayson was so proud of his son!

He loved Jenny just as much, even though he wasn't her biological father. He couldn't tell the difference, which was good, because Jenny loved him so very much! She was a big six year old girl now. She was very excited about having a new baby sister.

Meanwhile it's party time for Robby. He loves all the decorating the women are doing. He has to put in his two cents worth every now and then. Rachel lets him and Jenny help with the decorating, too. They finally finish and the room looks beautiful, but yet very boyish.

The invitations were sent two weeks ago. Rachel invited

several children from church, who were close Robby's age. Most were boys, and that would be a challenge... The day of the party finally got here, and everyone that was invited showed up. They all had such a good time. Rachel was glad when it was over, as she felt worn out. She was six months pregnant at this time.

Thanksgiving was just around the corner. Aunt Pat invited Rachel and her family to be guests at her and Roman's house. That would make things easier for Rachel, who gladly accepted.

Next was Christmas, with lots of shopping and holiday baking. Aunt Pat came over to help Rachel with the candy and cookie making. Since Rachel had invited Roman and her to spend Christmas with their family, she felt it was only fair for her to help out. Rachel had to admit, she was thankful for her help.

Grayson and Jenny helped with the Christmas decorating, for which Rachel was thankful. Everything was in place, and the log house looked absolutely beautiful.

Aunt Pat and Roman came over early on Christmas morning to watch the children open their gifts. There was so much laughter and happiness that day. It pleased all the adults to see the children having so much fun. They loved getting new toys, but the grownups realize that Jesus is the reason for the season. Jenny and Robby were too young to understand now.

Grayson will be reading the Christmas Story from Luke 2, after supper tonight. This has been a tradition every Christmas since Grayson and Rachel have been married.

Aunt Pat and Rachel were busy all day, fixing special food for their Christmas supper tonight. They would be having a wonderful meal together as a family. Jordan had gotten home from college a few days ago. He was as happy to get home, as Rachel and Grayson were to have him here. They didn't realize how much they would miss him. Jenny missed her brother, too. He had fit in so well with their family, and no one had any regrets how it had all come about. Again, God was certainly in the arrangements.

Jordan had gotten used to being Jordan Parker by now. He was happy to have his father's name. He felt so much at home with Rachel, Grayson and the children. He loved all of them very much.

Later that day, when supper was ready, they all sat down to eat. First they would thank God for the food, and the blessings he had bestowed upon them. They all had so much to be thankful for. After everyone had eaten, they sat around the table and reminisced. Each person was asked to name some things about their family that they were thankful for.

They started with Jenny. "I am thankful for my mommy and daddy... Aunt Pat and Uncle Roman... and... my new brother, Jordan, and... my baby brother, Robby. I'm also thankful for my baby sister in mommy's tummy." she said, with a big grin on her face.

This brought a smile to the faces of the adults. How cute Jenny was, they all thought!

Next it was Jordan's turn. "I'm very thankful for all my family! Without you, I would be an orphan. I love all of you very much, and will forever be grateful for all you have done for me. I am also thankful to have my biological father's name. Thank you Rachel and Grayson... for making that happen! Thank YOU, GOD, for allowing all of this to happen!"

Rachel's and Grayson's eyes filled with tears... as they listened to Jordan. He had brought them more happiness than he would ever know. What they had done for him seemed like such a minor thing, in exchange for all he had given them.

Next was Aunt Pat... "I hardly know where to start. I have loved Rachel ever since her birth. She became "my girl" at age ten, when her parents were killed. I don't think she ever realized how much she brightened up my life. I loved Mitch, then Jenny, and now Grayson, along with little Robby, and Jordan. I am looking forward to our new baby girl, who will arrive in a couple months. Last... but definitely not least... is my wonderful husband, Roman, who returned to me after thirty five years. Life is good... God has blessed me so much!"

Roman was anxious to tell what he was thankful for... "First I am thankful to God for letting me survive the accident, thirty five years ago. My life turned out different from what I had planned. I'm very thankful that I regained my memory... although I suffered the loss of Pat, all over again. I did my duty as a husband to my wife Julie, until her death. That left me free to search for my one true love. I am so thankful that God lead me to her, and that she was still single, and accepted the love I had for her. I love you with all my heart, Pat... and I also love all of you."

By now more tears were falling...

Rachel started her thankfulness... "I am so very thankful for all of you!" she exclaimed. "I love and appreciate Aunt Pat for all she has done for me. Without her, I would have been an orphan, too. I know she made a lot of sacrifices for me. She was always there when I needed help. She stood by my side through my marriage to Mitch and his death. It would have been so much harder without her. She was there for me through the birth of Jenny, and afterward. She has always been my mother, and I couldn't love her more. How excited she was for me, when I met Grayson. She saw me come alive again. She was there for me, no matter what I needed, and helped make this wedding perfect. Then when little Robby was born, she was there again. Aunt Pat... I can never thank you enough."

"You owe me no thanks!" exclaimed Aunt Pat. "I have loved everything I've done for and with you."

"I am so happy to hear that," said Rachel, wiping her eyes. "Now it's your turn, Grayson."

"I hardly know where to begin... "All my life, I had an image in my mind of the girl I wanted to marry. I never found her, until I met you Rachel. I knew in my heart that my search for love was over, once I met you. You were and still are, everything I have ever wanted. You are truly the most beautiful woman I have ever met and I love you with all my heart... now and forever. I am also thankful for all our children, and the one yet to be born. I thank God for bringing Jordan to us to love and to be our son. All of our children are blessings from God. I love you, Aunt Pat... you are also a very special gift from God! You have made so many sacrifices for Rachel and our family. We want you to know how much you are appreciated. We also love you, Roman. You have been here for us so many times, in the short time you have been back here. We're just one big happy family!"

"Amen to that!" said Aunt Pat.

The men and children retired to the den, while Rachel and Aunt Pat cleared the table and did the dishes. When they finished they joined the others in the den. Grayson had his Bible and was ready to read the Christmas Story. Everyone was silent while he read, even little Robby. It was a very sacred time...to listen to the birth of Jesus and reflect over the past years, and of how Jesus came to earth to live, and die for our sins. Grayson had such a wonderful way of discussing the birth, death and resurrection of Jesus. Rachel was so proud of him!

Chapter 31

Christmas was over and New Year's Day was here... It was the beginning of a new year. Rachel's baby was due around mid February. She was beginning to get miserable, and was tired quite a lot. I'm not as young as I used to be, she told herself. She tried to keep busy, and the time seemed to pass faster. Jenny and Robby took up a lot of her time, for which she was thankful. This seemed to make the days go by faster. She wanted this baby more than anything, but she felt relief when she thought this was the last time she would have to go through it. She was beginning to feel her age, although she was as beautiful as ever. She was glad Grayson had opted to have the surgery. He was such a wonderful man, and loved her enough to do anything for her. How could one woman be so blessed... to have two wonderful husbands in her lifetime? She had no answer, but thanked God everyday for her blessings.

Day after day passed, and Rachel was counting the days. She was getting more excited with each passing day. She and Grayson had decided to name their new baby daughter, Miranda Faith Sterling.

January passed and it was February now. Soon it would be Valentine's Day. That had always been a special day for Rachel. After Thanksgiving and Christmas, it was her third most favorite holiday.

Late into the night of February 13th, Rachel went into labor. When her pains were seven minutes apart, Grayson took her to the hospital. At exactly 2:15 a.m. on Valentine's Day, Rachel gave birth to a beautiful 7 lb. 12 oz. daughter. Miranda came into the world screaming. At least they knew she had good lungs. Grayson was with Rachel all during the labor. He never left her side. He was one proud father again. Miranda was a beautiful baby... She never had black hair like the other two... She had a head full of golden blonde hair... just like her mother. Grayson was so proud to have a daughter that looked like her beautiful mother. They were so blessed, to have such a wonderful, good looking family. He silently said a prayer, thanking God for all the blessings He had given them... Their four children. He was on top of the world!

Rachel came home a couple days later. Jenny and Robby were so excited to see their new baby sister. Of course, Aunt Pat was just as excited as the children. Even Uncle Roman seemed excited. He never had a family of his own, but he sure had one now, and he was happy for that. Life was good...

They were very busy raising the children, but never for a minute, did they regret having them. Jordan, Jenny, Robby and Miranda, had made their lives complete. The years passed quickly and the children were growing up. Jordan had graduated from college, and was working in the field of his dream, in Billings, Montana. He was happy to be near his family. He was in the process of buying a house in the city, near his job. He was engaged to a lovely young girl, named Haley. She was a registered nurse at the hospital near where he worked. They had met in college a few years ago. It looked as if there would be a wedding one day in the future. His family all liked her, and that meant a lot to Jordan.

Chapter 32

Jenny was fourteen years old now, and quite a beautiful young lady. She was very popular in school. She had a charming personality... like her mother. She wouldn't be allowed to date until she was sixteen, after her "coming out" party. That would be in a couple years. For now, all she could have were friends. The boys didn't seem to like it, but that was how it was. She understood and respected her mom and dad's rules. Just two more years, she thought...

Robby was ten and a big boy for his age. He was going to be tall like his dad. He was very sweet natured, and had lots of traits like his dad. He played all kinds of sports and was actually very good in each one. Rachel was so proud of him.

Sweet little Miranda was going on eight. She had grown up too fast! She loved school and was popular with her class. She was a real beauty, just like her mom... with long golden hair and those gorgeous green eyes. Grayson was so happy to see her looking more like her mother all the time.

Each of their children was special in their own way, and also very different. Rachel and Grayson kept the lines of communication open with them, and that was good. The children felt they could go to either parent, if they had something troubling them.

They had such a beautiful family, and thanked God every day for each one of their children. They were truly a blessing from Heaven! They thanked God and honored him by going to church every Sunday, and taking their family. Most every Sunday, Jordan would come over and go to church with them. Haley would come also, if she wasn't working. Rachel and Grayson were always so proud to have their whole family together. Sometimes they would all go out to eat after church, and sometimes they would go on a picnic on the ranch. Either way, they just enjoyed being together as a family. Life was good...

The family spent as much time together as possible. Grayson had bought three more horses, so Jenny, Robby and Miranda could ride with him and Rachel. This was a family activity they all loved. Rachel would pack a picnic lunch to take with them. They would always eat under the big tree, near the babbling brook, where their dad had proposed to their mom.

Somehow the subject of the marriage proposal always came up. It gave Rachel and Grayson time to reflect on the past, and be reminded of all the blessings God had given them down through the years. Grayson realized his life would have turned out much different, had it not been... 'FOR THE LOVE OF RACHEL.'

About the Author

Sally is the youngest of three children, born to Warren and Ethel Aker Campbell in Marion, Virginia. She is a Christian wife and mother. She and her husband Paul, live in the hills of southwest Virginia. They have 6 children and 7 grandchildren. Sally loves to write, do family genealogy, read and spend time with her family.

She and Paul are members of the Marion First Church of God, in Marion, Virginia. "For the Love of Rachel" is her second book to have published. Her first one was a Children's Fairytale, called "Princess Kari & the Golden Haired Boy." In 2008, she wrote her memoirs for her children, called... "My Life... My Children." She also wrote a short story called, "Memories of Dad." She is already thinking about a sequel to "For the Love of Rachel."